TO MATE A DRAGON

VENYS NEEDS MEN

NAOMI LUCAS

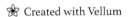 Created with Vellum

To Tiffany Roberts, Amanda Milo, and Poppy Rhys. Because you guys are the best!

BLURB

The human race is dying under the red comet soaring through the skies above...and with it, the sounds of dragons are in the air.

My name is Aida, and I was destined to lead the Sand's Hunter tribe into a new generation—promised to mate with one of the last born males along the Mermaid Coast. But before Leith was delivered to my tribe, my younger sister came of age and the elders chose her to be his mate instead.

Then a messenger came from the north with rumors of dragons turning into virile males from a single, human touch. Fresh hope blossoms within me as I plan to reclaim my rightful place as future matriarch to my people, and with that hope, I ready my supplies to hunt down one of these dragons to make my own. To touch him, to claim him, to take his seed and honor my people with a new generation.

But a storm is on the horizon.

And with that storm, soars an alpha dragon in heat. He's heading straight for me.

He sees me.

All my plans crumble under his dark draconian stare.

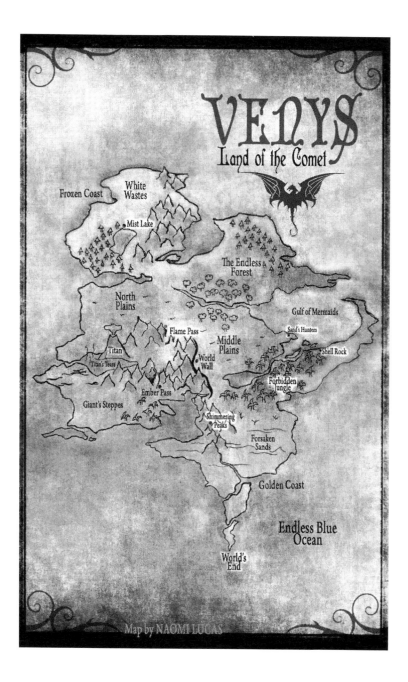

VENYS
Land of the Comet

Frozen Coast White Wastes

Mist Lake

The Endless Forest

North Plains

Gulf of Mermaids

Sand's Hunters

Flame Pass Middle Plains

Shell Rock

Titan

World Wall

Titan's Tears

Forbidden Jungle

Ember Pass

Giant's Steppes

Shimmering Peaks

Forsaken Sands

Golden Coast

Endless Blue Ocean

World's End

Map by NAOMI LUCAS

1

THE COMING STORM

Laughter fills my ears.

So much laughter. I long to join in but my sorrow weighs heavy on my heart. Everyone in my tribe is joyful but me, and they know it. They ignore my hurt because it's easier, and not wanting to be a burden, I try and ignore it too.

A breeze hits my skin, and a streak of red shines down upon me as the clouds move overhead. I glimpse the comet.

Many weeks ago, the red comet appeared in the sky above, lighting the land with a faint sanguine glow. A hush had fallen across the tribe as we gazed up at it, knowing its meaning.

Change. Wild, unpredictable change. That's what the comet means.

When it first appeared, long, long ago, even before my ancestors traveled to the Mermaid Gulf and settled down, joining with an established tribe already settled here, was the day the world twisted. Or so the stories go...

Our people didn't realize what it would do to us until many years later. But generation after generation, our peoples' ability to produce males diminishes evermore. Each generation is worse than the last.

This curse didn't only strike us, but the other creatures living across Venys. Many only produce female offspring as well. We know because our cattle are predominantly female and the merfolk say they have felt it too; though because they live long lives, many of their males are still around.

Now, the red comet comes every couple of generations to plague us anew. What will it mean for us this time?

Are things going to get worse? I sigh.

I check the ties of my net instead, testing them with my fingers. The net is not as large as I would like it to be—not for the journey I have planned—but it's the best one I have.

One thing is certain, I note, biting down on my tongue, pulling at the net. *A change is in the air.*

A week ago a messenger came down from the north, telling tales of a huntress finding a dragon. A dragon! A rare beast of old that my elders say they haven't seen since they left the wastes.

And sacrificing herself, the huntress went out to lure the dragon away from her tribe's hunting grounds. But when she went up to it—while it was slumbering—she touched the dragon's hide, and when she did, a fateful change happened. The dragon turned into a powerful, strong, human male.

I didn't believe it. No one in the tribe did... until the messenger said she was looking to invoke a mating pact with a tribe along the coast, for the child coming from the union of the huntress and dragon.

A rare male child, or so this dragon male proclaimed to the tribe he now lives with. Such a mating pact is a rare and special event—one that ties tribes together for generations to come.

It is not done lightly. It was then I believed.

After the messenger left, shrieking calls assaulted the land and the sky. The wails of a giant beast somewhere off in the jungle wilds bordering my home. Calls that my people have not heard since before my birth.

The calls of a dragon seeking a mate.

Perhaps... Maybe, maybe these dragons are the salvation for my people.

Which is why I'm preparing this net, planning to catch one for myself.

I have to try. If not to prove my worth to my people, to at least see for myself if this hope inside me is real. I will never forgive myself if it is, and I did nothing...

Giggles prick my ears. Looking up, I see Delina nearby in Leith's arms. He's kissing her neck.

A thorn of pain pierces my heart. Leith was to be *my* promised mate, the last male born in years on this side of the gulf. The brother of my best friend, Issa. She journeyed here not two days ago with Leith, delivering him for his mating ceremony with Delina.

My sister catches my eye.

Returning her smile takes a lot of effort, but I'm able to do it. But my lips crack under the pressure.

"Aida! Come and join us. We're heading to the nearby springs," Delina says, her tone heightened with pleasure. "This weather is making me sweat."

I stop rolling the net over my arm, pushing my worries deep inside.

Delina's curves, her long, dark hair, and her shadowed eyes of kohl are slanted with mirth. *She still wears the precious gold shells from her mating dress.* Leith is behind her, holding a basket of fruits, small pots, and folded cloths for drying. But it's my little sister my eyes linger on.

I'd wear them still too if I were in her place. It's an honor to wear the rare gold shells. *She's beautiful in them.*

"I can't." *For so many reasons.* I lift my arm with the net. "We need more fish for tonight's feast in honor of your mating," I say. "For the energy you and Leith will need in the coming weeks," I add thickly. It's not exactly the truth, but it's not a lie either.

Delina pouts. "Who will be our lookout if Leith and I rut?"

My nostrils flare, and Delina's mouth tightens, noticing. She knows I was to be Leith's mate, not her, but she pretends she doesn't—that she's forgotten my years of training, the honors and responsibilities the elders bestowed upon me.

When I don't give in, she sighs. "Fine. You're no fun. Leith will protect us anyway. Right, Leith?" she asks, turning to him.

He grins and shakes his shoulders, making the spear strapped to his back wiggle. "Of course. I have the biggest spear of all, and my aim is always true... and relentless," he answers lasciviously, eyeing my sister's skirt, where her thighs meet beneath.

Delina laughs, shoves him, and takes the basket from his arms.

Leith brandishes a bone knife before them and grips it in his mouth, pulling his spear out next—the weapon, thankfully —and jabs it several times in the air as if he's stabbing a jungle ape. More laughter follows, some of it from our tribemates nearby.

When Delina and Leith head off, bawdy jokes follow.

Watching them leave, the stiffness in my shoulders eases. I'm happy for my sister, but I can't help the sorrow within me. *What's wrong with me?*

Placing one hand on the net now rolled on my arm, one thought fills my head. *I'm the strongest, youngest huntress in my tribe. I've protected my people and our lands for years, showing my worth, exceeding the elder's expectations.* I straighten.

They may have taken Leith from me, robbed me of the future I dreamed of since childhood, but I will prove to them it doesn't matter.

I'll find a dragon, hunt him down, touch his hide... I'll seek my own mate to save my people from extinction.

It's what I've been born to do, what I've trained for.

Excitement fills me.

I'll find a mate worthy of me, of my people. My lips dare to lift into a smile.

I pivot back to the job at hand—preparing for the hunt—when I find my mother standing behind me, her face sharp with disappointment. My smile dies.

"You should've gone with them."

"I have chores to complete." I try to move past her before all my excitement fades. Before she can say more.

She grabs my arm, wringing me to face her. "And if they are hurt? Who will be to blame?"

"The tribe," I hiss. "Anyone can guard them. Why does it have to be me?"

"Aida! You are kindred! Leith is your brother now, and he brings power to our family, our bloodline. We are and always should be the first line of defense between Delina and Leith and the rest of the world. It is our duty. The tribe cares for us while we take on that responsibility!"

I jerk my arm out of my mother's grip. "It is not the responsibility I've trained for."

I know how I sound, I know... but I can't help it. I can't take on this responsibility yet. How much more do I have to prove?

"You are selfish, daughter. You are one of the strongest left among us. You should be honored with this new path."

Flinching, I take a step back. And there it is, the reason I can barely make myself laugh or smile. It's not because Leith is no longer mine—I don't even find him all that attractive—but the discarded sensation I get every time Delina or my duties—my honor—is brought up.

"I should be honored, shouldn't I?" I say. "But you make it hard for me to feel anything but rejection." She opens her mouth to argue but I cut her off. "I have given my whole life for my people. I have done everything you demanded—I have become strong and capable, foregoing childhood fantasy because the elders deemed me a match for the last male born along the Mermaid Coast. And now, Delina does nothing but come of age, and she is given something I have worked so tirelessly for. With no explanation but *'she appears more fertile, has childbearing hips.'* I should be honored, but I cannot make it happen."

"Aida..." Mother's face falls, and that hurts me worse than her disappointment.

"Don't, please." I pivot to walk away, unable to bear her any longer. "Give me more time. I need time," I say hurriedly, heading for the lift down from the rocks to the beach.

"Aida!" she calls after me, making me wish there was an easier way to escape. "I know you are prepping supplies."

I stop at the lift's lever and wrench my eyes closed.

"I know your head is filled with fancies of dragons," she says, cutting into my excitement. She walks up behind me, her hand taking mine from behind and squeezing it. "I know you're preparing to go out and find one for yourself. Face me, daughter," she urges.

Turning back around slowly, I do as she says, all while knowing what is about to come.

She lets go of my hand and cups my cheeks. Her voice lowers. My heart cracks. "I know we have hurt you, have dishonored you. I know having Leith taken away to be given to your sister is not an easy thing to accept, not when you've been told your whole life that he and you were destined."

Unable to look away, I drop my eyes.

"I wish the elders could have spared you. I wish Delina had an ounce of empathy to show you, but don't you see? Can't you see why we decided to make Delina Leith's mate instead of you?"

"You think she's more fertile," I whisper harshly, feeling a little jolt of anger rise within me.

"No, Aida," my mother says, leaning in close to whisper in

my ear. "You're worth more to the tribe with all your strength, with your courage and tenacity. Delina... well, Delina can barely lift a spear or create an ointment for pain." She lets out a little laugh. "Let her be weighed down in pregnancy for all the years to come, not you, my dear daughter. As I, your cousins, and the other dying families grow older, we will need your strength to survive. We will need you as you are."

She's trying to make me feel better, but instead, her words only make things worse. Mother was a great huntress and guardian, even while she was pregnant with me and my sister, and Delina is more capable then she's saying.

I know Delina's worth. As my sister, she is worth my life.

Yes, Delina lacks empathy, but she's strong-willed, and an incredible cook. Her fingers are dexterous and she stitches the most beautiful shell jewelry and hide coverings. I love my sister and mother—even when she tries to cow me—as I love the tribe.

But this... I don't need this, whatever this is.

Mother is focused on the tribe as a whole, and not the whims and wants of a single member, not even if that member is her own daughter. I can't blame her.

It's people like her that keep us alive.

"Yes, Mother," I say, all I can say.

She smiles. "Good. Now, stop this nonsense and be the Aida I raised. The Aida your sister and Leith need, the tribe needs." She lets go of my cheeks. "I'll send Milaye to guard your sister and Leith while they bathe, but next time, I'm sure you will make the right choice."

I watch Mother walk away, back toward the central bonfire where some of the other older women sit around cooking.

The clouds shift overhead, streaming red down upon the village in waves, shadowing sections in red and brightening the rest with sunlight as they move over the comet and sun above at different times. I catch the gazes of some of the tribeswomen, and they glance away at once. But I don't feel shame knowing they heard everything my mother said.

No, there is only numbness in me right now. Numbness that allows me to think.

Instead, I look back up at the sky, out towards the ocean to my right and over the cliffs of my home. I notice darkness begins taking over the sky.

The clouds are not friendly puffs but one long miasma that shadows the usually twinkling blue ocean into a somber grey. It's hazy in the distance, making the sky and ocean become one. It's rain, lots and lots of rain.

I frown.

I hope Issa made it home to Shell Rock. I think of my friend who promptly left after delivering her brother here to return home. Thunder hits my ears.

And with it, an ear-splitting roar.

My muscles tense, and my palms slicken with sweat as a shiver streaks through me. Birds ascend into the sky, fleeing. Another scream assaults the air, one after another.

They're closer.

So close, the screams vibrate my bones, my soul.

Glancing at my mother, she's looking straight at me, her expression worried.

"Storm!" someone yells. The rest of the women get to their feet in a flash.

A drop of rain hits my cheek. Without another thought, I rush after Delina and Leith.

2

THE DOWNPOUR AND THE DRAGON

DRENCHED IN RAIN, I race over the rickety wooden bridge that connects the cliff of Sand's Hunters home to the jungle. From there, I stumble down the slopes to the west that lead to the springs.

Within minutes of that first raindrop, the tribe fell into chaos. The clear skies of the morning vanished under clouds that gusted over our home, bringing with them an angry and wild surge of wind.

Following the path, I see the small waterfall up ahead that pools into the basin in the rocks, water that will eventually lead into the gulf. But it's the deep cave beneath the pool that makes it a spring, and the water fresh and unsalted. A private, beautiful place hidden by large rocks and tall trees with sweeping leaves.

Branches shake and lower with the rain as Delina and Leith come into sight. Naked, under the falls.

Delina is against the rocky wall as Leith thrusts into her. My mouth drops.

I come to a stop next to Milaye, the tribeswoman guarding them.

"We need to go!" Milaye screams from the shore, but neither Delina or Leith hear her. Milaye flinches when she sees me. "They can't hear me from under the falls," she huffs.

Rain plops down on both of us as she says it. "I'll get them. Go back to the tribe! They need help getting everything inside."

She nods and jogs up the path. I pivot back to my siblings...

"*Delina!*" I shout, waving my hand, getting no reaction or notice from my sister.

A streak of lightning sparks through the canopy and without waiting, I dive into the water and swim to them. Under the falls within seconds, I grab Leith's shoulder and tug him back.

They meet me with muted screams and one boyishly shocked expression.

"What are you doing!?" Delina cries, shielding herself. Leith wades back. I keep my eyes high.

"There's a storm! A bad one. If you heard Milaye shouting for you, you would know. We need to get back to the village now!" My voice strains under the din of the water. I swim back to the shore without waiting for them to argue. Grabbing one of the hide towels they brought with them, I wipe myself down once. When I turn, Delina's behind me tugging on her clothes, Leith doing the same. My eyes don't stray because it's apparent he and Delina didn't finish.

"It was so nice a little while ago," Delina whines but grabs her basket.

Leith picks up his spear. "It'll be nice again. Let's go. The tribe will need us," he says. And with that, we head back.

When we get to the bridge, my mouth drops in horror. It's thrashing from side to side, and on the other end, anything not bolted down is blowing in the wind.

Leaves from the trees fly everywhere, the rain has turned into a full-on downpour, and the lift is crowded with people as they head down with supplies and animals. Below us on the beach, there are others rushing inward to the sea cliffs bordering the jungle, and to the caves a short distance inland that becomes our shelter in emergencies.

"We need to get across!" I scream, looking back up. Milaye is on the other side of the bridge, facing us, with her sisters Ola and Panyia.

Thunder resonates.

"We'll hold this end. Leave the basket behind!" she shouts across, wind chasing her words.

"Delina, you go first," I say, taking the spear from her. "Leith, you follow close behind. I'll go last."

My sister gulps and nods, and I see her shake through the rain gathering in my lashes. She grips the rope handles with white knuckles and takes a step forward.

"I'll be right behind you," Leith tells her. Delina nods and slowly makes it across.

"Go," I tell Leith when Delina reaches the end.

"You should go first."

I shake my head. "No. You are far more important. You are needed—our salvation. I'll hold the ties on this end. You have to go first."

"Aida..."

Forcing a smile. "If you die, I'll die anyway," I say lightly. "The tribe would never forgive me."

He nods stiffly but his brow is furrowed, worry in his eyes. He turns to the bridge and grips the handles, white-knuckled like my sister. "You'll be right behind," he calls to me.

"Yes." I hold the ties.

Leith nods again and makes his way across, stopping whenever a gust shakes the bridge. When he makes it to the other side, I sigh in relief.

My turn.

Grabbing the rope for myself now, I hear snapping as a

single fierce gust swings the bridge. Taking a step onto it, I'm immediately thrown to the side.

I hear a scream but don't look up, trying to remain calm. Holding strong, I ride out the shift, focusing. When it levels, I move forward, one step at a time.

Another crack slices the air, joined by thunder. I halt, waiting.

Glancing outward, my mouth dries up. I'm midway. Only midway. The bridge sways side to side. My feet shift and part.

Lightning fills the sky in vibrant flashes. A spark of heat whips through the wind when a terrible erupting boom fills my ears. I see one of the trees in the village sizzling, split in two. Milaye covers both Delina and Leith with her body, forcing them to the ground.

Screams ring in the air.

They look at me with wide, horror-filled eyes.

"Go!" I shout, "Get to the lift. I'll be right behind! I promise."

Milaye nods resolutely and I'm thankful. Delina starts fighting but Ola grabs her and forces her away. Leith lingers another moment, catching my gaze, and I take another step forward. He turns away and runs after Delina.

Only Milaye remains to hold the bridge for me. Now, swinging back and forth, I'm practically hanging on, using my feet as leverage as my arms do all the work.

I see some of the tribe staring up at me from below on the beach.

"Aida! Don't stop," someone yells, and I drive forward, pain ripping my shoulders, jerking my arms this way and that to get to the end.

I miss my final step, but Milaye grabs me, pulling me into her arms, and we tumble to the ground together in relief. But we have no time to celebrate.

In the next instant, we're running to the lift. Delina and the others are below. We begin cranking it back up as Ola and

Panyia run with Leith and Delina down the beach, under the gape where the bridge swings, and toward the caves.

As we wrench the lever, I realize Milaye and I are the last ones left in the village. The rest have already fled to safety. The underlying scent of burnt wood floods my nose.

And then I hear it, a different sort of roar. Not like the screeching one from before...

It's so loud, so much closer than any other, so terrible it nearly stops my thrumming heart. My hands stop cranking, and Milaye takes over as I peer out to the east, down the coast, over the turbulent waves where the sound resonates from.

In the direction of Shell Rock and Issa's home.

But it's so much closer than that, my thoughts tangle, fearful. *It's right there.*

Right there.

Coming through the veil of rain.

It goes on and on, over the thunder, joining with flashes of lightning, pounding my eardrums, taking me over, solidifying me to the spot. I can't tear my eyes from the horizon, knowing it's growing ever closer. My heart lodges in my throat. My fingers twitch.

"Aida! We must go!"

Milaye says something and grabs my arm, pulling me onto the lift. My eyes tear away from the horizon. The roar continues.

"Aida, what is happening to you?" she snaps. "Help me with the lever. It's sticking."

It's enough to shake me out of my reverie. Just as the dragon's roar ends.

Together, we release the sticking lever and loosen the ropes for our descent. The lift starts lowering, but Milaye rushes her side, and we jerk down at an angle. Catching up to her, I straighten us out, knowing it's fear that's driving her.

It should be driving me too, but it's not. My veins are full of the lightning that's in the sky, of wild adrenaline, and not even the aching pain in my wrenched muscles can overpower the thrill surging through me.

A dragon made that sound. I steal a glance back to the horizon.

I see a shift, a giant shadow.

Before the lift hits the beach, Milaye jumps off and runs toward the cave, vanishing around the rocky outcropping that makes up the base of our home. I take a step to follow but stop, staring down the coast. I cannot resist.

Something dark moves in the rainfall, something large, menacing, and far more astounding than anything I could've imagined. It's not coming from the sky or the land, but from the water, emerging like a tidal wave to curve downward and disappear a moment later.

Water rushes over my feet, the waves building higher and crashing, moving farther inland than any storm has taken them before. Still, I'm rooted to the spot. But the shadow vanishes and it's enough to bring my senses back.

Run! My body urges me suddenly. *Go!*

I pivot to the lever and yank it until the lift is above my head.

And when I turn back around, the shadow is no longer a shadow, but a dragon in all its beautiful, frightening glory coming straight for me.

3

ZAEYR SURFACES

Yes.

The hollow cry resounding in my watery cave makes me alert. A femdragon is in heat, is in need. And she's close to my abyssal territory where I horde my treasures. I hear her, though she is above the surface, crying for a male to seed her and give her a dragonling.

It is what I have been waiting for. A female to bring to my nest, to covet and protect. Offspring to raise and expand my domain.

Though listening to her cries, so far away, I soon realize they are from above the surface, and not the yowls of another water dragon like me. I had always planned to breed with another of my kind, to share my sapphire and pearl caves with her, but no matter, a rare female is nearby, and she will be mine.

Mine. The word is strange in my mind. *Mine...*

Slipping through my underwater system, seeking one of the exits to the sandy bottom, another, more infuriating cry reaches my sensitive ears.

A male roaring in response to my female. A male who does

not know better. *I am an alpha water dragon! An alpha of ancients, king of this trench, ruler of the turquoise depths, and guardian of the deep!* Any alpha or beta male within miles will know of my stirring, as I sense theirs. *They should be afraid.*

This femdragon is mine. I have claimed her. Even if the other alpha dragon gets to her first, I will fight him off her—slice him open with my talons, and take his place mounting. I have waited too long for a femdragon in heat to enter these lands just to lose her to another!

Clawing my way from my glittery caverns, my patience flees, discovering cave-ins where I have failed to maintain the area over the years. *A serpent like me does not leave his home on a whim*, I snarl, baring sharpened teeth at the rocks.

The male's roar echoes, fueling my frustration, my longing to breach the surface and inhale the femdragon's mating pheromones that are sure to bloom the air for miles in every direction.

I wonder what she smells like...

Turning my head to the side, I peer through one of the many holes from which light streaks from far above into my caves, contemplating the barrier holding me back. My tail overturns shells, rocks, and jewels as it scours the bottom of my deep cavern. A low growl escapes me, releasing stores of oxygen in my gut and forcing bubbles up through the hole. Watching them rise, I see a shadow swim overhead, and then another, and another.

Mermaids.

More bubbles escape me in surprise as a boulder is moved over the opening, right before my very eyes.

Quiet accompanies my shock, as one by one, all the holes that give my dwelling light are closed off. I twist around, making the ground tremble. I peer up through the last one left until that too closes off.

The mermaids are trying to trap me in!

Sea snakes, villainous wretches!

This is how they repay me? For leaving them alone, allowing them to settle within my coral reefs and valleys? For protecting them from vicious, hungry deep-sea monsters that would love to dine on their flesh?

Worst of all, the echoing yowls of my future mate and my competitor are gone. *I've waited centuries for this.* Loss hits me harder than it should. Loss and anger—rage ignites.

How dare they? I dig my talons into the stony floor of my domain and pull my wings inward, upward, shelling my back. *They think they can keep me trapped?*

My body fills with lava-like heat, erupting with my quaking emotions.

Nothing will keep me from what is mine. *NOTHING!*

I ram my back upward.

The ceiling cracks and stones and dust falls around me, polluting my cherished home. I ram my back again, and more gives way. Terrible, hollow sounds fill my ears, eclipsing even the thunder of my furied heart.

I do not stop, and even when the rocks and sand bury me within, I keep hitting the cave ceiling with all the might of my body. Pain tears through me. The weakest parts of my wings scrape and rip as my body becomes compressed. But each time I thrust up, cracks form—it is working. The trench terra shifts, and slowly, far too slowly for my liking, the pressure on me gives way.

Hours turn to days, and my body is nearly empty of all its oxygen stores. My limbs are numb with exhaustion. I need to surface soon. Desperate, giving a final shove, the ground below me loosens. The remaining rock and sand fall upon me, around me, under me where a deep crater forms. Renewed with the seabed's movement, I slam my tail up and break through. My wings and body quickly follow.

Sunlight—red light—fills my view.

I am free! I open my long mouth and roar. My body revels and shakes with ferocious delight.

The ground sinks beneath me, caving in. I swim upward into the open water. The once mountainous seascape crumbles and vanishes around me. Water *whooshes* past my hide and under my scales, falling into the terra below. Coral reefs collapse, and colorful schools of fish scatter every which way.

Sharks swim away; octopus scurry from the budding cracks. *My creatures flee because the merfolk sought to contain me.*

Part of me is sad for the loss of my home, my treasures and jewels, for the space I hoped would one day become a nest to share with my mate, but the other part is dead set on one thing: finding the femdragon in need and making her mine.

My shaft emerges from my body, rigid and ready—and large, my potent seed brewing forth, ready to fertilize.

Feeling it drag beneath where my tail meets my body, my eyes focus through the light I am not used to—not anymore—and scan the blue waters of my home for mermaid traitors. *They have fled,* I notice, seeing none around me. *Good.*

Taking no time to hunt for them, I swim toward the direction my femdragon's sounds came from, picking up speed as the dappled sunlight and glow of the cursed comet disappears in the waters. Everything moves out of my way.

Days, I realize, *I have lost days escaping from my caves.*

And then I hear it again, my femdragon. Heat grows in my belly all over again.

The water is gray and dark when I emerge. Clouds fill the sky overhead. I inhale air. Rain falls upon me when I glimpse the shore and the edges of my territory.

Kaos's territory. Now I know who my adversary is. A jungle dragon bred from a water and earth dragon long ago. *Like I was.* We are similar in age, he and I. We respect our borders and have never had a need to fight.

All these thoughts fall from my head as his and my femdragon's pheromones fill my nostrils.

Not even a storm could remove them from the air.

Hot, mossy, potent, and rich. Subtle in the winds but I smell them, hating Kaos's scent as much as loving the femdragon's. My large body contracts with need, my talons descend, my wings strain and seize. I dip my head beneath the water to cleanse the chaos in my mind, only to reemerge to scream at the world, my eyes on Kaos's jungle.

FIGHT ME! All the power of my soul erupts in the air, louder than thunder and higher than the crashing waves. *Meet me and fight for mating rights!* Smoke plumes from my mouth, saying as much in challenge.

My eyes go to the jungle's edge as rage builds, where a lone figure is standing on the shore. A human. Throwing all my intensity her way, she retreats back into the shadows of the trees.

"FACE ME, KAOS!" I bellow in dragon. "Come to the edge!"

I do not want my future mate near us when we battle. Blood will spray.

But minutes pass, and Kaos does not show. He does not answer, and my mind grows curious in its chaos. Seeking him out with my senses, I find I no longer feel him.

My opponent is no more, though his pheromones remain on the wind.

It cannot be. My nostrils flare. Tearing my eyes from the shore, I look ahead of me down the coast, straining my sensitive ears for a telltale sign of my brethren. *He cannot be dead. I would smell that as well...* But the femdragon comes back to mind, and all thoughts of Kaos fade.

And then I realize it.

Humans. Distant screams flood my ears. *Human shouts.*

Protect my female at all cost. Slipping back into the water, I follow the noises down the coast, to the source of the damning yells.

If they have touched Kaos, then my mate is in jeopardy. *I will not lose her,* I vow. Not after losing everything else.

I will not.

4

FACING AN ALPHA DRAGON

STILLING, I feel the blood rush from my face. My heart nearly jumps from my chest, and my throat closes off as my mouth opens. Rain hits my face, falling over my brows and into my eyes. I reach up and wipe them only to lose sight of the giant beast swimming toward me. And when they clear... he's just that much closer.

Hazy gray swathes of rain are all that lies between us, and without looking, I know there's no place for me to hide. The lift wouldn't help me escape. Only the beach spans out before me, and the rocky cliff-face behind me has no outcroppings or rocks for me to hide behind.

The jungle is far above, and so are the giant broken-off land masses my village rests upon.

I'm stuck. Out in the open, exposed. And though my body screams for me to run, I can't move.

I can't lead him to my people, who are surely in the caves by now. Delina, Leith, and Milaye are probably just as exposed as I am as they head there.

No... I swallow hard. *I can't run.* My hands clench at my sides.

The dragon heading straight for me is nothing like the beast the messenger spoke of. Her story depicted an enormous brown and bronze dragon, with leathery wings, deep amber eyes, and scales covering its huge body from tail-tip to snout.

She said it looked like it belonged in the wastes, colored by the terrain it slumbered in.

No, this one is nothing like that dragon at all. I gape.

This water draconid is something straight from the colorful reefs and the turquoise ocean on a clear, calm day. And with each second, it gets closer, and more of its details appear. Awe and terror hit me all at once. My fingers twitch at my sides. I stiffen further, muscles locking.

A long serpentine body slips in and out of the waves, making waves pound upon the shores violently. A tail that goes on and on follows and sways behind the body, getting lost in the riotous water as much as its causing it to be that way. Sapphire-like scales cover whole sections of its body, and deep ridges ascend from its brow to crown its head in a myriad of opaline colors.

A dangerous, sharp-edged jewel of a dragon is before me, so beautiful and terrifying all at once that it could make me cry if numbing adrenaline hadn't already taken me over first.

It lifts its head to the sky and bellows, and I'm finally able to move, stumbling back. Flinching, I cover my ears with my hands. A walloping shriek tears from its throat and two massive silver-blue wings snap from its body, shooting upward as its body rears back to rise from the waters.

Like its long tail, the dragon's wings are so large they could destroy my entire village in one thrust. They fill the sky, the horizon, and one gust from them is strong enough to lay me flat.

My butt strikes the sandy ground as a wave careens over me. Gasping, I scramble up and backward, blinking out salty tears to the higher ground on the beach.

Making it to semi-dry land, a fallen spear washes up next to me. Grabbing it before it's lost, I pull it close, turning back to face the dragon.

Glowing blue eyes pin me to the spot. My once thundering heart stops. The dragon's long head is forward, pointed in my direction. *And those eyes...*

A soft cry of fear tears from my throat. *His eyes are on me. I'm going to die.*

How did I ever think going after a dragon was a good idea?

But even as I'm thinking these things, other, more primal sensations course through me. The word *fate* hits me, making me shake.

I watch open-mouthed as its body lowers, its webbed toes and talons—which will soon shred me in half—dropping back below the waves. But it's not until it rushes straight for me that I turn and run, making it a dozen feet before a hot gust of wind slams my back. My wet hair flies forward as I catch myself before I fall. Another breath, and a growl sounds in my ears.

Gripping my spear tight, I pivot to face the sea-jewel dragon and face my fate head-on.

Long, sharp, glistening teeth meet my eyes, baring at me, shielding a forked tongue behind them that swishes from side to side. Smoke bursts from between its teeth to rise into the air, flooding my nose with brimstone and ash.

He's not more than several arm-lengths away from me, my mind reels. Why doesn't it attack?

The dragon's jaw snaps closed, and my gaze shifts to his bright, glowing eyes. The saliva in my mouth dries up. Small blue pupils stare daggers back at me, surrounded by brilliant blue light.

The dragon exhales another breathy gust. Its heat washes over me, and for a moment, the rain is gone from my flesh; my eyes dry up—I blink—it's gone, and I'm drenched again.

"Go on with it!" I yell. "Kill me already!" I take a step forward.

Thunder slices the air, lightning flashes across my periphery, and somewhere far off, I hear the cracking and destruction of trees.

Yet the dragon just stares at me.

But then a thought pops into my head.

I don't have to die.

I'll live if I can touch it.

The rain beats down hard between us as I assess the space between us, as I wonder if I'm fast enough.

My toes curl. Suddenly, everything in me wants to touch this amazing creature, enough that it nearly hurts. My hands are twitching again.

Does he feel this too?

"Dragon," I whisper, having no idea if he'll hear me or even understand me. There's so much I want to say, so much running through my mind, more sensations crashing through me than I can understand. All that comes out is, "I need you."

Not, "Please don't hurt me." Not, "Make it quick."

Not, "I don't want to die."

I *need* you.

I take another step forward.

A noise emanates from the dragon's throat, and it's nothing like I've ever heard. Ancient and thick, and it falls over me like the heat of his breaths. A whipping sound hits my ears, and his giant silver-blue wings span out to cover the sky above my head.

My lips part as I begin to raise my hand into the air between us.

And right before I close the distance, nearly touching the sapphire scales of its sharp jaw, a familiar shriek assaults me, and rage darkens my dragon's bright eyes. Falling back with a scream, he rises, lightening his backdrop, as he swivels his head to the left.

The ground shakes, and I twist onto my hands and knees and crawl away. Another, much smaller, dragon lands; it's black and wet and glistening. It sees me and yowls, clawing its way straight for me before its front legs even touch the ground.

Chaos erupts as I scramble to my feet, preparing to run, but the large dragon jumps onto the smaller one, pinning it down before its jowls touch my flesh. Wings, tails, claws, and limbs slash the sand near me.

I dodge and fall, zig-zagging between, trying to get away. Every time I'm about to be crushed or hit though, I'm not, and begin to realize the larger dragon is shielding me.

My feet sink into the sand and waves crawl over my flesh, as I aim for the ocean, hoping to swim away. Then—hearing it more than seeing—one of the dragons slams into the cliffside of my home.

A tail stops me and I pivot to the side, forced to back up onto the rocks, using my spear as leverage to keep me upright.

Twisting further, I thrust my spear toward the fight, toward the water dragon's wings and its back, its tail lashing the air above my head. The smaller dragon flaps higher into the air, claws elongated and stretched, and latches onto my dragon, curling its long tail around the bigger dragon's body. The black dragon's eyes catch mine—there is only hate there—and its jaw opens, thrusting its head over the larger one's shoulder and biting down on its wing.

Red blood sprays everywhere.

A cacophony of sounds joins the constant thunder and my blue dragon rears up and drops down on the smaller one. The black one tries to climb out but is stopped, grabbed by something I can't see, and pushed to the sand. It doesn't try to escape.

I don't see the smaller dragon at all.

This is your chance! I glance to either side of me but only see the storm's waves to my left and falling rocks to my right. With no other exit, I give into the chaos, the inevitability, and stumble forward, raising my free hand to place it on the large dragon's back.

An electric shock rips through me, pushing my eyes to the back into my head. Dropping my spear, I place my other hand on the dragon, suddenly needing more contact, finding a ridge on his wing to clutch. Without deciding what I should do, I press my whole body against him, shaking with bliss.

It's the last thing I know before I'm shoved to the ground and my world goes dark.

5

ZAEYR LOSES ALL

PINNING the femdragon to the ground, my mind roils with mating heat. She sinks her talons into my hide, through my scales, and rends my chest, my shoulders. "Submit," I demand, growling down at her, snapping my jaw.

But her eyes are wild and all she wants is the human woman behind me. Her pheromones surge off of her in devastating plumes, only to be swept away by the wind and rain. Though they fill my nose, I retain clarity.

I do not want her to hurt the mortal woman, I realize as I continue to keep the femdragon away. At first, I thought I did not want her to touch the human, for fear of losing her, but the longer I protect the woman... now I do not know.

It is the human woman in my head, the way she stood up and faced me, the dark of her eyes as she looked at me head-on with nothing but a stick in her hand.

The femdragon screeches and a lick of fire hits my neck. "Submit!" I order, needing time to understand what is happening.

Why am I not satisfied to have the femdragon beneath me?

Why am I not biting her flesh, laying my claim, and turning her over to mount her from behind?

"They stole my mate. A human stole my mate—she stole my mate!" the femdragon hisses and screams.

"I am your mate," I growl.

"My mate," the femdragon cries, slashing and twisting to get out from beneath me. "I burn! She stole him from me!"

My anger turns to fury, jealousy.

The human female is Kaos's? *It cannot be. I did not smell him on her.*

Anger builds within me. It is the human female with long, dark hair—wet and curling in the rain—blustering in the wind that steals my thoughts. *I did not move when she reached for me. I did not swallow her whole or burn her with fire...*

He is not even here! Has he taken all from me before I even escaped my watery cave? Blood red thoughts rip through my mind. I thrust the femdragon down with one claw as she tears back into me.

Flaring my nostrils, I do not even smell him on the femdragon.

Nothing is stopping me from laying my claim...

I allow the mating heat and her pheromones to build, to take over the rest of my thoughts—forgetting all else—even Kaos... when something touches my wing.

Leaning over, I open my jaw, ready to force the femdragon to finally submit, thinking nothing of the touch. Instead, I focus on the feel of her serpentine body loosening.

Yes. This is right. This is my prize.

But the touch on my wing grows almost immediately, stopping me right before my teeth descend. Something presses on me like a warm sea flower.

My body stills, my talons curl. The femdragon beneath me begins to fight again, wailing her anger.

I no longer care. Not certain I ever cared.

My wings tighten, I shake them, and my tail lashes out to remove the thing on my wing, dislodging it in one swoop. The feeling remains. And to my shock, it spreads up the nerves of my wings, to my spine, down it and over my tail. Every muscle clenches, stimulated by the strange sensation.

Hot and cold, zips of fire and threads of ice. I try to shake that off too but my body disobeys, weakening. Devastating pain slices through me, everywhere, from my soul outward, from my slashed chest to my head drumming with electric shocks.

Lifting my head to the stormy sky, I bellow as lightning rains down around me. It strikes me, igniting my insides with world-fire.

Losing my hold on the femdragon, she swipes at my neck and hisses, getting out from underneath me, and ascends into the sky.

With one last bout of strength, I slam my wing into her and slam her into the cliffside. Howling in pain, she quickly rights herself and flees from the spears of lightning trying to zap her down like a bug. I lose sight of the femdragon in the clouds and collapse to my side.

Thoughts of the human woman return.

And it is with those thoughts my body begins to twist and break.

My spines fall off, falling out of my skin like needles, leaving holes in my flesh. My hide shrinks and my bones splinter, popping out, only to diminish and fall from me. I cannot roar anymore; my throat is closed. I try and flap my wings, but they are cinched and weak.

My head hangs heavy, and I drop to the sandy beach, paralyzed with shock as the ocean crashes over me.

I remain awake, forcing it, as the world grows bigger, all while a picture of the woman with dark hair, her hand almost upon my face, remains with me. It is that image that keeps me from darkness.

Revenge, the idea of vengeance, clouds that moment. *It is because of her that I am breaking... It is because of this human my curiosity was driven to the brink.* I have destroyed my cave for a femdragon I didn't mate. I have lost everything I waited for. Wanted dearly.

Soon, a single wave drenches me wholly, completely, and the salt of the water finally loosens a growl of torment from my throat. It leaks into my wounds, stinging.

I have new hands and long legs; I am cold and wet. So much pain, I squint the water out of my eyes, and rising, stumbling on hands and knees, I try to brace myself on soft, weak feet. But waves rush me again and again and I'm forced to crawl farther onto the shore. Only when I reach the sand do I peer down at the place on my chest that burns. Blood trails from deep wounds that have yet to close.

Thunder rumbles, and it is quieter now in my new ears. Wiping my eyes, I find my sharp draconid vision gone.

But I notice a shape on the sand ahead of me, moving stiffly, using the cliff face to stand. It stumbles but rises again.

The human.

She is turned away from me. Long, wet black hair is plastered down the curves of her back, her rump.

"You," I growl. My anger builds, seeing her.

She does not seem to hear me. I claw my way toward her without her noticing. "You," my voice lowers. I feel this human to my very core. I am privy to her struggles and the bruising on her flesh.

It hurts, but I ignore her aches.

Right behind her, I rise and grab her wet coverings. I lose my balance and we fall to the ground. She yelps. She kicks and struggles but stops when I tug her under me and straddle her body.

She is much smaller than me, her strength no match for mine even in my new form. There is pleasure at the thought. More pleasure than having the femdragon would have given me.

Her eyes widen to dark beautiful orbs, fluttering shut from the rain. My body stiffens. Her lips part. Her gaze runs up and down my face and body.

"You," I rasp. "You have taken everything from me."

Her eyes narrow and I focus on them, missing her stick as it comes up and slams into the side of my head, knocking me out.

6

AIDA DRAGS HOME A DRAGON

"WAKE UP!" I yell, standing over the male who's out cold. I struck him impulsively, not thinking what I would do next. He doesn't stir.

Guilt settles deep as I look upon what I've done. One minute, I was facing two battling dragons, trying to survive—the next, they're gone and a frightening large manbeast has me under him. *It is not my fault! I was protecting myself.* Yet the guilt grows.

Leaning over him, I cup his face and urge him to get up, but there is no response.

Noticing gashes over his neck, shoulders, and chest, I curse. They're gnarly and exposed in this weather, and with the lightning continuing everywhere, I begin to worry for his safety from the storm. Bright light flashes over his form, and my mouth drops.

It's just your head, I tell myself. I know I hit it and lost consciousness at some point in the mayhem. But I can't deny the long silvery blue horns coming from the male's head, or what looks like a scaly tail rising from his lower back...

Nor his nakedness. My eyes widen and I glance away,

33

searching for a place to go before the tide reaches us. Though the image of his solid, erect cock imprints on my mind... how it lies against the wet sand.

If I doubted he was the enormous water dragon I had touched, I believe now.

Squeezing my eyes closed and rubbing my brow, I push the image away. It's wrong to check him out right now.

I hear a low moan and my eyes snap open. His fingers reach for his neck.

In a rush, I pull off my top, ripping it down the back, leaving only a tight band to cover my breasts. Then, using one of the sharp shells adorning it, I tear it into strips and bind his wounds as best I can.

I get most of his neck and part of his arm covered before I run out of hide. He's still moaning.

"I'm so sorry," I murmur, trying not to touch him more than I should... even though I long to run my fingers over his muscled arms and chiseled chest. I want to so badly my heart pounds relentlessly. Warmth swirls in my belly. "I hope you can forgive me."

Glancing behind me once more, I know if we follow the rock wall bordering the jungle, we'll eventually reach the caves. *The cliffs will provide protection from the lightning.* It's a way to go, but we can't stay here, not with the coming tide. *We could be underwater in another hour.*

Peering back at the male, I know I'm going to have to get him to safety on my own. It's the only way. I can't leave him here to die.

Getting up, I take a deep breath and grasp his hands.

And with every ounce of strength there is, with desperate adrenaline rushing through my limbs, I begin to drag him through the sand.

Minutes pass by like hours, and the chill of the rain vanishes with exertion. I pause to shift his weight—grabbing shoulders or shifting the way I pull, minding that his bindings stay secure—but I don't stop. Every time I glimpse the beach, the water is a little closer. Each inhale is excruciating, and when I hear flapping, cracking sounds above me, I find we're under the rope bridge. It's broken, and the ends slam the walls with each new gust.

Gulping, I turn away, heaving the male along. The cliffs go inland from here.

It feels like an eternity has passed, but we finally make it to the grassy rise before the cave's entrance.

The lightning has lessened without me noticing.

Another deep, straining moan reaches my ears.

Stopping for a moment, I drop down beside the male and check his wounds. My hands still at their discovery. *The bleeding has stopped... The shallow ones are nearly closed.* Licking my lips in wonder, I take his hands again and lug him up the final rise.

When the rain stops falling, I know we're under the cave entrance's cover. I collapse at the male's side. Catching my breath, my muscles crying, I peer out into the storm and realize it's almost nightfall.

The storm's been raging for hours.

He groans; I moan. Everything hurts. Now that we're safe, the pain hits me tenfold, and minutes pass before I can even consider moving.

The warmth in my body worsens instead of cools. Pressing my hands to my chest—I gasp—swearing there's smoke rising from my mouth. Eyes widening, wiping them several more times just in case, I exhale again, but this time there's no smoke. Moving my hands to my neck, my pulse vibrates erratically under my fingers.

What in the waters was that?

Storms, dragons, a beastly male... and as if the male knows my thoughts, he groans. I turn my head to the side, taking in his outline.

A huge beastly male, I correct.

Sitting up slowly, I lean over him and my sex clenches. Frustration guts me. I shouldn't feel desire, not now, not like this, but my body has its own way of handling the stress of the situation. My sex clamps again, harder this time.

I nearly died several times over. I curse.

But then again, I nearly die every day while out hunting. The fact that I haven't proves my prowess to the tribe, my ability to provide, take care of others, and lead.

Staring at the dragon male, I remember *his* prowess and strength on the beach, his glowing, knowledgeable gaze and that enormous body that filled the sky... It all returns to mind at once, exciting me. My body startles. *He was so strong.* Still is. I take in his dangerous-looking horns.

Horns, yes. Sharp, long, and pointy, they're jutting from above and behind his ears. The same color as his scales were.

Are, I correct myself. He still has scales.

His shaft has teardrop scales that look like velvet.

A deeper heat grows inside me. *Aida, you pervert.* I shake my head.

He has long white-blonde hair with pale blue streaks throughout, but it's hard to be sure with how wet it is, the way it's damp against his skin.

Then there's his body, long and toned with muscles only the strongest hunters have, but bigger still. Because he's long— taller than anyone I have ever known. Taller than me by a head or so, taller still if I include his horns.

Gaze traveling down to his tail, I barely comprehend it. Mermaids along the coast have brightly colored fishtails, and the dangerous jungle nagas have snake tails, but this male is no mermaid or naga. He has legs. Legs with thighs and calves that beg me to run my hands over them because they are sculpted to perfection.

And though I try hard not to look at his cock, I can't help

but see it out of the corner of my eye. My strange internal heat bursts when I finally allow myself another glimpse of it.

A blush rises on my cheeks. *Oh, waters, is he endowed.*

I know he is because the elder males and females of my tribe—those who are or once mated—talk about rutting often, often with giggles and jokes, telling stories of when they were young and there were more partners to be had.

I've heard them all, even the fake ones of phantom men coming from the Forbidden Jungle to ravish our women late at night, or those of male merfolk who loved to slide their tongues between our female's legs—because mermaids only have a cold hole, they complained...

Or some of the tales the grandmothers would relish telling: the dumb, burly giants, lugging heavy clubs between their thighs, that *their* mothers and grandmothers had once encountered in the wastes and played with.

The dragon male's velvety scaled cock could be considered a club too. A club that's smooth and rigid like the rest of him, partially blue, partially silver, with veins pulsing and a tip that's twice the girth of his shaft. And his girth...

My hands twitch. I don't know if I could grip him, not with how bulbous his shaft is... though I'm curious to try.

My sex flutters again, unwittingly, feeling emptier and needier than ever before. I grump and run my hands over my face. I need this dragon man now. *Right now.* My chest tightens as something primal threatens to take me over.

Another streak of guilt hits me. I force my gaze from his cock and steady myself. Again. What is wrong with me?

Pressing my thighs together, I rub my face harder, only looking again at him when I know I've gathered control—I won't jump him while he's unconscious. Untoward sexual encounters are a sinful act among all the tribes and are harshly punished.

His tail twitches, catching my attention.

It couldn't have been comfortable having it dragged through the sand. Biting my bottom lip, I check his wounds again, peeling back the makeshift bandages.

They're still raw and deep, but like the shallower gashes, they're practically healing before my eyes. I notice nowhere on his body—which is nearly silvery white—is there a slight bruise or tiny scratch, not even a rash from being hauled through sand and over small rocks. I'm thankful for this.

Glancing at myself, I know I'm bruised before even seeing them form on my dusky skin.

"Aida! You're safe—oh my..." I hear Milaye's voice from down the cave passage before I see her. She comes to a sudden stop several feet away, eyes widening on my dragon male. "Oh my..." She mutters some more in shock.

"Help me," I groan, sitting up straighter, jealously covering him from her gaze. I hate the idea of her seeing him. He's mine. I sense it deep inside where the heat in my chest has yet to leave. "He's hurt. He needs help."

He's mine.

She nods and runs back into the cave. Shielding his nudity with my body, the strange possession continues to build. I wrench my eyes closed and rest my brow against the male's, praying to the waters that he doesn't try to kill me when he wakes.

7

DRAGON DESIRES

I GET the male settled on a cot near one of the cave streams inside, upon a natural platform by the cave wall.

A bend in the stream ensures our privacy behind a rocky wall, enough to stop most of the curious gazes of others—and they *are* curious, anxious even, some frenzied. This spot is ideal for the sickly and hurt, with the shallow pool next to us and the trickle of a spring deep behind the rocks for fresh, clean water. It's a good spot overall.

Luckily, most of the tribe has bedded down for the night. No one else is hurt from the storm.

But those who remain awake and watchful are staring at me and mumbling with others, presumably about me and the new male. Within minutes, their curiosity drives me to find a couple spare hides and erect a makeshift wall to keep their roaming eyes at bay. The beach cave is big, long, and goes on for multiple sections, which spreads us all out. I'm thankful for that because I need privacy more than anything else right now...

I look around, seeking security in this new location, and see there are some ledges higher up crowded with emergency supplies.

When we lost a portion of our village to a hurricane shortly after my birth, Sand's Hunters lived here until they rebuilt the village. Since then, this place has been maintained, a place of safety if ever an event like that falls upon us again.

Torchlight is flickering, lighting up the cave. The sounds of thunder are distant now. I peer down at the male resting before me.

Or a dragon... I swallow, staring at him. His eyelids flicker but they don't open.

Pulling my tangled, wet hair back and tying it in a knot with some rope, I settle next to him.

"Aida," Milaye says softly from beside me, peeking over the hide. "You should get looked at by your mother, she wants to see you. Let me take over or allow one of the healers to tend him."

The male groans. But it sounds more like a growl to me.

I won't leave you. I don't think I could even if I tried. My body loses its warmth whenever I step away from him.

Using a wet cloth and clay bowl, I begin cleaning the male's skin. "I'm fine."

"You could've died. When I realized you weren't behind me... and saw that monster down the coast..."

Glimpsing Milaye's face, I see guilt and sadness. I give her a reassuring smile. "You didn't leave me. I stayed."

She frowns. "Why?"

Shaking my head, I force the smile into my voice. "I had too. I needed... I wanted to make sure that whatever came wouldn't follow me to the cave. The tribe, you, Leith, Delina, are my responsibility."

"I would never forgive you for dying on my behalf," Milaye says indignantly. She studies me, the male. "You wanted to see if the monster behind the rain was a dragon," she accused. "Guess he was."

"Yes, that too. I stayed for several reasons," I answer honestly with a shrug. "Regardless, even if it had been a disturbed kraken or a giant serpent, I wanted to make sure it followed me, away from the cave, and not you. Luck gave me a dragon." I turn to the male, whose brow is furrowed now. I reach up and smooth it out with my cloth.

A hush settles over us, and I know Milaye is staring at me.

My sister's voice breaks the silence. "So the messenger was speaking the truth? Dragons can be turned into humans?"

Looking back up, Delina's face is now peeking over the hide next to Milaye's and both their faces are exactly the same, eyeing the male. Annoyance fills me even though I can't blame them, knowing I probably have the same look when I stare at him. *Good thing he's draped in hides from his waist down.*

Though there's a tent where his erection is...

"Is he..." Milaye pauses. "Is he the beast from down the coast? Is he a—a dragon, Aida?"

The male groan-growls again, and my eyes snap back to him. I begin unwrapping the bandages from around his neck, hating the half-dried blood and dampness keeping them stuck to his skin. "Yes," I say, wondering at the question myself. Though I know it has to be. The silver-blue water dragon vanished and in its place, *he* turned up. *With a tail, horns, and sapphire scales.* "I think so, yes," I mutter, throwing the strips of my old shirt aside.

"Oh my waters," Milaye gasps. "I knew it."

Delina jumps. "I knew it!"

"You got yourself a dragon, a male. Aida, it's a miracle!" Milaye's words flood my ears with excitement and dread. *They didn't see him, didn't see his violence, his might. I don't know if he'll kill me when he wakes up or try to leave... or both.*

What if he leaves without killing me first?

Delina scoffs. "Just because Aida brought him in doesn't mean he's hers. The elders decide who is the best fit for a mate. The best female will be mated with the best male."

My heart sinks. *She's right.*

"Even if that's true, you're already mated, Delina," Milaye snaps. "You won't be considered."

"I'm the chosen female!"

I urge them to lower their voices but they ignore me.

"And what about Leith?" Milaye gripes.

"It wouldn't be my choice," Delina says with a whine. "It'll be the elders' choice."

"Stop!" I nearly yell. "Both of you," I continue, lowering my voice. "He's hurt and needs rest and proper bandages. Your squabbling isn't helping. We don't even know who or what he really is, or if he'll even stay. Maybe he already has a mate."

"I can stay and take care of him. You should rest," my sister says, beginning to move around the hide barrier.

Milaye grabs her and pulls her back. "Oh no you don't." Delina whimpers, grasping at Milaye's hand. "We all know you're terrible at healing. Let's go tell the others still awake and worrying. I'm sure Leith is looking for you, and there's plenty of food left to be passed out."

I catch Milaye's eye and mouth *thank you.* She smiles and drags my whining sister away. But a moment later, Milaye returns with a bone dagger in her hand, offering it to me.

"What's this for?"

"Protection," she says almost too softly for me to hear, her eyes going to the male. "He may be a male, but you are a sister to me. Be diligent."

Overwhelmed again, I take the dagger from her and hook it into the ties of my skirt. "Thank you," I mumble.

"Hollar and the tribe will be here in a flash," she says.

I nod, having not given a single thought to finding a new weapon. My mind has been on many other things. Milaye stares at me for a moment before turning and vanishing behind the makeshift walls.

Peering back at the male, my mind reels. *Finally, we're alone.*

But what if he does harm someone here besides me? *I won't let that happen,* I admonish, touching the dagger once with my fingers before dropping my hand.

I notice his face is turned slightly toward me now when it had been facing the cave ceiling before. I frown. His eyes flicker once behind his eyelids.

"Are you awake?" I whisper.

No response.

Hmmm.

"Are you faking it?" I ask next.

Still no response. Squinting in curiosity, I soak the cloth with water and focus on cleaning his wounds. His neck appears under the blood and grime, and I discover his once deep cuts nearly gone. Feeling for a pulse, finding it strong and hardy, I lean back to take him in.

He hasn't twitched a muscle, I note.

I keep cleaning his body, moving down to the gashes on his shoulders and chest. They're all red and tender but closed. Swiping the blood away that's gathered, I go to rinse my cloth again. When I check back, I swear the tent where his cock's heaviness is springing up stands higher.

Gulping, clenching, I dart my gaze back to his face and chest.

He's a gorgeous male, beautiful but robust at the same time. Every part of him is honed and sculpted, from the tips of his spiraling horns down to the glittering hard scales and the claws on his toes. I want to grasp his horns and squeeze them—rub my fingers and palms up and down their lengths. I want to taste the sharp slash of his lips.

He's almost too deadly for a human, any human, even while sleeping. But something pulls me to him despite knowing he could hurt me, break me in two. That he could wake at any moment and throw me to the ground.

He radiates virility, rawness, and strength. Everything that is prized in the tribes. That I prize.

Whoever—if anyone—gets to be his, they will be the safest, luckiest, most envied woman on the Mermaid Coast. My hands shake a little as I scoop out healing ointment to slather and massage onto and around his wounds, my thoughts trailing to the dagger Milaye handed me.

I hope I don't need it.

The male groans, deep and guttural.

My blush returns in full force and I swallow thickly, already frightened he'll be taken away at any moment.

I could handle him.

I could try.

I want to try. I'm excited to try. My body tenses, and my core flutters at the prospect. I've waited years to mate, suffered countless nights of longing...

And that right there, I realize, is why I'm feeling so lost.

Delina is right. It's the elder's choice. Mating has always been the elder's choice since the comet's curse.

She is the chosen female... Why do my thoughts go there? They only emphasize how confused I feel, feeding the toxic mixture of fear and envy running in my veins. My fingers and palms rub the male's skin almost worshipfully. *This may be the only time I'll ever touch him.*

I can touch him while cleaning him...

His lips part and a quiet moan escapes him. I nearly moan in response, wanting to so badly lie down next to him, curl into his side, forget all these thoughts, and for once, in years, feel at peace.

I imagine it, as if all my training, all the responsibilities the tribe has put on my shoulders since childhood, pretending it could all be pushed away—even for a few minutes—imagining that I won't have to live to see the gradual extinction of my people.

That I'll have someone strong beside me when things get too hard to bear...

"I know you may be sleeping," I say quietly so no one else would hear. He spoke my language before I knocked him out, but that doesn't mean he'll fully understand me. "I know you may not get my words, but if you are the dragon on the beach, I want you to know—I want you to know that I was going to search for one of your kind and see if the rumors of dragons turning to men were true.

"I wanted to believe, you see, *needed* to believe. But I didn't think it would actually happen, and if it did—I doubted that I would even have the chance to touch you, never mind that you would even transform. But now that you're here and I can't deny it, all I feel is guilt. I'm confused. So confused. I hate these gashes on your flesh, and I can't help but think it's my fault. I'm sorry. If you want to hurt me for what I've done, I understand. If you want to leave, I will make sure no one stops you. I'm sorry."

With my mind going back to the dagger hooked in my skirt again, I continue, "It's my fault you're here, not the tribe's. If you want to hurt someone, hurt me, not them."

Desire builds within me at my words to prove myself to this male. Prove to him that I'm not a bad person, that I will honor my words and him. That I will take the blame and not hide. That I will fight for my tribe, and I will fight for him.

Because as I'm watching his wounds close shut, and while I'm spreading his hair out on the hide untangling his knots, I can't help but know that my touch upon his wing changed my life forever.

And his too.

8

ZAEYR IN HEAT

AIDA. The human's name is Aida.

The other humans call her that. It is nearly all I can think of since I heard it. *What a strange and simple name.* Though as I test it in my mind, I find I'm liking it too much—fury should be the only emotion brewing within me.

"Please forgive me," Aida says again. I hear every word she utters.

She asks for forgiveness. My thoughts will not go there.

She acknowledges her selfish act for touching me too, I note. I am almost awed by her honesty. *She is sorry for the hurts on my flesh...*

Does the human female not realize she isn't responsible for these gashes? That the femdragon did it in her frenzy?

The rends to my skin are nothing, not even fatal. A battle wound well taken.

This human could never hurt me in such a way, it is almost laughable to think of.

But when she falls silent, I quickly realize how much I was enjoying her voice.

Aida. My mind tastes her name again. Waiting for her to

speak, I am annoyed that only her soft breaths, trickling water, and the distant talking of other humans greet my ears.

I have been awake for a while, pretending, listening in on my new surroundings, deciding whether or not these humans are a danger to me.

Waiting. Waiting and figuring them out, waiting for my strength to return. My new form is as strange to me as Aida's name, and I need to get a sense of it before a battle ensues. *If* one ensues.

Aida reassures with her words.

She does not know me! A tendril of anger returns. *She will pay for what she has done!*

As her hands caress my neck and clean my wounds, my instinct to enjoy her touch tries to overpower the fury in me. *I like her touch.* I like being touched. It is so rare for me to touch another; I have forgotten what the sensation feels like. I bask in it, wanting more, wanting her to press upon me and have her everywhere at once.

She has no idea what confusion feels like, I groan inwardly.

I know I still retain scales, but even they are far more sensitive than ever before. And the places where my flesh is exposed, a terrible and hungry stirring blooms. I could become addicted. A short while ago, I was in the most pain in my life, and now... Now, I am enjoying pleasure unlike ever before.

My need for revenge grows—to shove her to the ground and finish what I started, to make her pay for her crimes, to kill her and destroy this perverse bond she has forced upon me.

To subdue her, bite her, mount her. A growl tears from my throat as I consider touching her intimately, of her hands returning the favor... the thought takes over the death plans.

She is sorry! She asks for forgiveness!

The longer I wait and listen and learn from her, the more I am coming to understand death is not what she deserves.

She deserves punishment. She says she will accept it! My brow furrows slightly.

If the human bond is what my ancestors have warned me of... *Her death will result in my death too.* And I can sense the bond, the tying heat that already connects us. It is in my growing need for her presence.

The thought of her death should give me pleasure—like it had for an instant on the beach—but it does not. Only vengeance does now, vengeance and having her by my side. Inconveniently incompatible ideas.

I do not want this human to die.

Mating, mounting, taking this blasted ache in my loins will be her punishment. And when the mating frenzy is gone, I will deny her my protection and a nest of my making—as she has denied me my hope. She will never be rid of me, and she will suffer it for as long as we both live.

I force myself to calm down and relax before I give myself away.

But I stiffen when the human female pulls my hair out from under my head. *I have hair!* She runs her fingers over and through it, avoiding my new horns, upending my thoughts again.

I want her to touch them, for her to feel their power. But her fingers twist in my strands instead and my scalp prickles deliciously, sending shockwaves of pleasure straight through this new body of mine.

Every moment in her presence makes it harder for me to pretend I am unconscious.

Sensing her lean over me, I tense further. *If she is under me, she cannot escape me or her punishment.*

I am ready to mate. Human or otherwise, my body is primed, and will not find relief until the act is complete.

Her soft breath warms my brow. I inhale and take her scent into me.

She smells of warm sands and sweet jungle spices, of fresh rain and ferns. So unlike the smell of any dragon that I have ever encountered, fem or otherwise. And it has been so long, so long since I smelled anything.

Aida's scent eclipses all others, even the femdragon's.

"I don't want them to take you away from me," she whispers, pulling my thoughts back to the here and now.

Take me away from you?

Them? These elders the other humans spoke of?

My anger returns, slicing through me like talons. The petulant words of one of the human female's return. *'A chosen female,'* she said. *'The elders decide.'*

No one, especially humans, will decide anything for me. They would not dare.

My eyes snap open when Aida's head settles on my belly. I try to keep my body from going rigid, but my cock spikes upward. Lifting my head, I look down at her, pulling my lips back into a snarl. But as time passes, she eases upon me, and I know she has fallen asleep.

My chest swells, watching her. I ache to take advantage of her slumber and familiarize myself with her body. *My bonded human's body.* The thought makes my shaft twitch—finding the deep place between her legs where it will soon invade. Filling it at my leisure while she is so subdued, I imagine how soft and accepting it would be... while she is weak with sleep.

A plume of wispy smoke leaks from my mouth.

Femdragon's remain open for their chosen male until their seed has taken root. Would it be the same for humans? But as the night lengthens, I keep my thoughts in my head; the distant chatter stops, and I suspect I'm the only one left awake.

Aida sighs, shifts onto her side, and nuzzles my stomach. The sensation makes me growl, and her body stiffens against me.

The female human snaps upright, her dark gaze widening as she finds mine. The blue glow of my irises reflects in the sheen of her tired eyes.

Her chest rises and falls. "You're awake."

"Yes."

She scoots back when I sit up. I grab her, pulling her arms before she scurries any farther away from me. Her whole body strains under my grip, her mouth hanging open.

"Do not scream," I warn, my voice darkening.

Her mouth slams closed.

My fingers tighten around her arms with warning as I draw her to me. To my surprise, she does not struggle.

When I have her where I want her—locked against my chest, facing me, her legs pressed to mine—I round one arm over her back and lift my other hand to grasp her neck. My aching shaft rests between us, and with a final shift, I pull her close.

The pressure of her body, so near yet caged behind these wretched hides and armor layers between us, makes me want to roar and rage.

No femdragon hides her sex.

If this human submits so easily, her sex should be open and ready for me. But as I think this, her eyes harden. *Not fully submitted, I see.*

Interesting.

My fingers shift, settling on her throat. It moves and quivers.

"You say you are sorry," I begin.

"You *were* awake! I knew it."

Snarling, she goes quiet. "You ask me to spare your people, but not spare you, why?"

She licks her lips and the hardness of her gaze softens—a little. "If the stories are true and a touch from a human turns a dragon into a man, then I stole your life from you."

"It is true," I say, unable to keep the relentless anger from my voice.

She flinches. "I know that now..."

Silence falls between us as I stare hard at her face, enjoying this slight body of hers, so powerless in my arms. There is a dagger on her hip but it does not bother me, in fact, I would like to see her fight with it. It would make her punishment all the more enjoyable.

But tendrils of wet hair fall from the thick knot of hair on her head, framing her face, teasing her skin. With my hand resting on her neck, I notice it is shades darker than my own. *Like the inner tones of conch shells,* I muse, petting her throat with my fingers now. *Or the coral reef sands right after sunset.*

I see her better now than I did on the beach, back when she defied the terror my large form should have given her and brandished her spear instead. I see her bright, honeyed eyes in the torchlight—near gold and amber in flickers—gaze into my own, framed by lashes so thick and curved, all I can think of is one word: sublime.

Pulling her further toward me until her chest is pressed hard to mine, I wonder at human breasts as I look down at the cushiony orbs squeezed between us. My fingers strain where they rest on her waist, wanting to feel them. *They are soft,* I note, *her butt is soft on my thighs where she sits on me.* Parts of her are so soft while the rest of her is toned. I caress her waist with my fingers. Her muscles shake beneath them.

"Are you going to hurt me?" she asks, a barely-there whisper. When I glimpse her face, her lids have lowered and the skin of her cheeks has taken a deeper hue.

My lips twist and stop my caressing. "Does it hurt for a human to be mounted, subdued, taking the mating heat of her mate that she so unwittingly touched?" My shaft jerks between us. I admire its size a moment, pleased how similar it is to the appendage I had before. It is heavy and tight, and I can feel my potent seed enlarge my balls. *Seed that she will take!* My prick was heavy when I was a dragon, but it is heavier now.

Aida quivers against me, rubbing my cock with her movements, driving me closer to madness.

My voice lowers. "Does it hurt being pumped with seed, bitten, and rutted, not only to answer for your crime but to take the punishment you offered so sweetly to accept? Does it hurt knowing that the only forgiveness I will accept from a human wretch like you is relief? Relief from this ache in my loins, relief from this new body, satisfaction from your submission to all my whims, and a brood of my own that I have wanted for more lifetimes than you have lived or will ever live?"

Her nails dig into the scales of my arms, her hold on me tightens. Her lips part. A rush of her pheromones floods my nostrils, burning the heat I'm barely keeping at bay. The need to sheath my cock inside her sex and spend my seed builds.

"I—I," she stutters, jerking back, rubbing me while she does so, forcing the dangerous tension inside me toward the brink.

Releasing her neck in a flash, I grasp her hips to throw her on the floor so I can mount her from behind.

The next second, I am on top of her, throwing the hides aside and ramming my hips against hers, trying to find her deep. It's hidden among the tussle of her weak armor. "You will take me again and again, human! That is your punishment!" I hiss.

Pulling her hair to the side, I force her to look back at me.

"Aida!" a voice calls out, interrupting as our eyes meet. I snarl loudly in warning. *Death will come to those who intervene!* I thrust my hips forward, my cock tip finally hitting—finding—the soft, wet heat between her thighs. It slips before it fully penetrates her.

"Mother," Aida gasps loudly, throwing herself away from me.

My hands drop. *Mother?*

Aida scrambles away and rises.

9

THE ELDERS

Before dawn, I'm led deeper into the cave, following a path of torches to where the elders are. Mother leads the way, huffing, upset.

She's horrified that the male was awake, shocked that he was on top of me naked—I'm reeling from that too—and concerned for my safety along with his. She didn't want me alone with him, and now she's made the sentiments known, loudly, for all the nearby tribemates to awaken and hear.

I'm upset too, but for so many reasons. My body is doing strange things, and my thoughts are a mess. My core hasn't stopped fluttering for hours, and my arousal gathers to trickle down my legs.

He was nearly in me. For a moment. The shock of that has yet to leave my body. Truer aim, and my innocence would have been taken. Snatched. And claimed.

My mind and my body have yet to decide how I feel about that.

I keep rubbing my thighs together, trying to make my arousal go away, but it just gets worse. I've never been this aroused before, not even while thinking of my darkest fantasies late at night...

And it's worse because *he's* behind me, not a stride away, often daring to come closer and breathe down my neck. I can see his shadow eclipse mine now and again as we walk, and the dark sharpness of his horns pierce every gloomy corner. Even with a pelt tied around his waist, I feel his cock poke my backside every time he bumps into me.

I brace for his brutal penetration constantly.

He bumps into me a lot. To the point that if we had nothing shielding us right now, I'm sure he would have no problem rutting me while we walked, in front of everyone... slipping his shaft between my buttocks with each stride.

My core gushes a little. More uncertainty knots my belly. I imagine it. Then there's a twinge of shame and embarrassment.

Milaye's sisters are following behind, weapons at the ready, I remind myself. *Stop thinking about sex.*

And if that wasn't bad enough, my stomach is grumbling, my limbs are tight from abuse, and the restful, amazing sleep I got lying against the male—whose panting in my ear is making my spine ramrod straight, my whole body aware of his—wasn't nearly enough.

Around us, people waking for the day, and the first wafts of cooking fish fill the air.

My face falls. *I don't want to face the elders.*

Not now. Not like this. My dewy thighs slip against each other with each step.

Mother stops before a large tent and turns to me. "They have questions, Aida, for you alone," she adds, glancing at *him* behind me.

He growls, steps up right behind me so that we touch, and I pivot to face him. "It's the law of the tribe," I urge, peering up at him. Every time I do so, my gaze goes to his glittering horns.

"I do not care for human law," he utters.

Mother tugs me back, brow furrowed and flashing him a look of annoyance. "My daughter saved your life, tended your wounds, and has given you shelter. Soon you will be fed. You will obey our laws while you are a guest here, male. Unless you forgo our shelter and choose to leave?" She sounds hopeful.

His gaze mutes when he looks at her. "Leave? No, I will not leave, not yet," he says. "But make no mistake, human, your daughter owes me a great debt. One night of shelter does not begin to cover what she has stolen from me."

Mother's mouth purses. "Go, Aida. Talk to them. They're waiting. Your father is waiting. I will stay here with—what do you call yourself, male?" she asks.

The light briefly returns to his eyes. "Zaeyr," he announces, straightening.

"Zaeyr," I whisper. He turns to face me, flashing me a look of ferocious desire. *Zaeyr.* I like it. I like it so much more than any other male name I've ever heard. "Wait here," I say quickly. "I'll be right back."

I'm forced to bear the weight of his heavy stare before I turn and duck through the tent entrance. A sliver of coldness runs through me as I walk to the central fire and face the two men and two old females before me.

Nata and Drea are the last of the grandmothers. Nata is a great-aunt to me, my oldest living relative since my grandmother passed away years ago. Stagie and Tabach are the last of the old men.

Though Tabach is my father, he is twice the age of my mother. His first mate could not conceive children, and after many years of failure, Tabach mated my mother, Shyn, when she came of age, producing me and my sister, who she raised with the tribe's help. They do not live together, but they are amicable. Mother takes care of him in the elder huts where he now resides.

There are two other males in the tribe, but while they are

far from young, they are not considered elders. Milaye's father and another, each produced only female children. Oled, Nata's son (and one of the very few males born here in the last generations) was sent to Shell Rock many, many years ago to keep the bloodlines pure. Shell Rock is where Leith was born and his elder sister, my best friend Issa, will one day become matriarch.

"Sit, Aida," Nata tells me. I drop to my knees with a winded sigh. I'm too tired to care about anything except what they say and getting back to Zaeyr. Nata's brow furrows, and she hands me a loaf of bread and cheese. I bite into it with gusto. "You know why you're here," she asks.

I swallow. "Yes."

"You brought a strange male into our caves," Tabach says. "A male with substantial life-threatening wounds we've been told."

I set the bread down. "He's healing. His wounds are almost gone now. He's awake."

The elders glance at each other. "How?"

But before I can answer, they argue.

"Is it true he's a dragon transformed? Are the rumors true? Awake you say?"

Nata quips. "Dragons haven't been seen in these lands since before I was born!"

"If he's a dragon, will he harm us?" Drea's croaky voice stops the others.

Holding up my hand, I try to answer, but Tabach levels me with a look. My father and I don't speak often; in fact, he's only a father to me in name. But when we do talk, I'm intimidated.

He may be old, but he's still strong, and his voice still holds that strength.

"Daughter, did you encounter a dragon in the storm and touch him?" he asks.

"Yes, I did."

Silence descends as their gazes fall on me with wonder.

"What happened?" Nata inquires.

Inhaling, I tell my father and the others what happened, starting from the bridge to the dragons clashing on the beach... But after that, I keep some of the details to myself. They don't need to know about the overwhelming sensations I get whenever Zaeyr and I touch. Or my obsession with him that only grows and grows...

Even now, with thick hides and yards between us, I feel him as if he's sitting beside me. I know he's not, but I'm colder now sitting next to a fire then when my body was warm next to his.

The elders glance between each other again.

Father faces me. "The messenger that came from the north mentioned a bond... Have you... are you *bonded*?" he trails off.

Flushing, my chest tightens. "I-I don't know." I don't want to tell them. I can't lie, though. If I mate Zaeyr—which almost already happened—they'll all know that there is something between us. "There's something, something that happens when I'm near him." I gulp.

Nata squints. "Which is?"

"My body grows very warm and comforted in his presence." It's not the entire truth but it's enough. That I'm wet and achy between my legs and half my thoughts are about finding relief —*that* I keep to myself.

"Do you think he feels the same?"

"I don't know. I'm not sure I'm comfortable asking..."

"He speaks our language?"

I nod.

"Hmm," Drea grumbles, rubbing her chin. "If he is unmated, I wonder if he would accept a female from our tribe and join with us."

My chest squeezes painfully.

Tabach interjects. "We would like to meet him. You say his wounds are healing and he's awake. Do you think he is strong enough to face us?"

I open my mouth to answer when the tent flutters behind me, and there's a chorus of collective gasps.

Zaeyr's voice resounds before I can twist around. "I am strong enough to face anything, let alone humans."

He doesn't think much of us. My hands ball into fists. But he moves to stand behind me and when I look up at him, his gaze flashes hot and heavy towards me before pinning the elders. My back straightens as the rush of heat returns. Holding in a gasp, it's almost too much.

My mother rushes in behind him. "I'm sorry! I tried to stop him!"

"It's okay, Shyn." Tabach coughs, rising slowly to his feet to welcome Zaeyr by the fire. Shyn goes to his side to help him. "Please join us—" he hesitates "—dragon, and sit."

"No."

10

SLEEPING WITH DRAGONS

IT SEEMS like half the morning has gone by before I'm able to leave the tent. I'm a shaking, confused mess.

Hoping to question Zaeyr in private, the elders asked me to leave on several occasions, but Zaeyr refused to stay without me. After the third time trying, they stopped.

Milaye's sisters are long gone by the time we emerge and have been replaced by others with spears and bone knives. Zaeyr grips my arm, making the female guards tense, but nothing happens when I allow him to lead me away. Stumbling from exhaustion, he catches me and keeps me upright, making me lean into him for support.

I hate how good it feels.

But I sense my father's scornful gaze on my back as we leave.

Despite all our time talking, the elders refused to accept there's a bond between us. And because Zaeyr would not say one way or another, he left me alone to justify my body's dire response to him while they talked and talked. It hurt. I hurt.

At least he refused to leave my side, even when Drea offered him a place in our tribe and a mate of the elder's choosing, promising peace between our species and for children bred from his loins.

Zaeyr made it clear—shockingly, embarrassingly so—that he would take who he pleases, and no one, let alone meddling old humans, would tell him otherwise.

The elders don't like their power denied.

They didn't so much as look at me, mention me, or bring me up at all except for his transformation. It was as if I wasn't even there, wasn't even considered...

I don't get it. *What have I done?*

We enter the main cave, and I look around to see half the tribe is gone, fires burnt out, and those who remain are carrying supplies back out. *The storm's passed,* I realize and head for the exit. Zaeyr's hold on me tightens, stopping me.

"No. You need sleep."

"I should be helping my—" Glancing up at him, I know there's no point arguing. He leads me back to our spot up on the ledge, hides us from intrusive eyes, and I lie down. I hear him growl at the guards but once my head hits cushioned hides, any cares I have left cease.

Sleep overtakes me immediately.

Blissful, peaceful sleep.

Sleep that ends all too soon when I wake sometime later breathless and sweaty, with my legs open.

Heart thundering, gasping, I sit up, only to be stopped by a large body and large hands. They grasp my shoulders and force me down. I nearly scream. Peering wildly up through the darkness, Zaeyr's glowing blue eyes light the shadows between us.

The torchlight is near gone.

We stare at each other. His hand slides up to cup my throat in warning. I swallow. He pets me. Swallowing again, I realize I'm completely naked.

And wet.

"What?" I whisper. "How?" Nervousness ricochets through me.

His gaze narrows.

"Your elder humans do not choose for me," is all he says. He leans down and licks my chcek.

Shocked, I go rigid.

He got my clothes off while I slept. And the wetness, I realize, *the wetness is on my skin.* His tongue laps at me.

I know where the dampness came from...

Zaeyr is like a nightwalker, plucking out my most ardent, hopeless fantasies, and offering them up. A sliver of fear tears through me, fear for what's happening, but also mindless, quaking excitement.

"To defy them," I force out as the hot slide of his tongue tastes my face, my ear. "It could mean exile."

His teeth graze my lobe. "Dragons nest alone."

Shivering, pressing my hands to his shoulders for space. He gives me none. "Are you choosing me?" I ask.

He rises to meet my eyes. "We are bonded, human."

It's not what I asked, not what I want to hear. My heart sinks a little. "I choose you," I tell him honestly.

His gaze darkens and he rises further. A chill drifts across me from the distance. "You touched me, human. You stole my immortality and my great form. I was an alpha! An ancient!" His voice rises. "I ruled the gulf in its entirety. And now... now other dragons, lessers, will come in and take it and there is nothing I can do to stop them! I was feared by all, and now I am human, a weak creature."

I push him off me and sit up. "Humans are not weak. *I* am not weak. On the beach, you didn't pull back when I reached out to you. I needed to touch you and I think you wanted me to and would have let me if the other dragon hadn't come. You were just as entranced as I!"

He growls, his eyes flash brightly, and smoke trails from his mouth between us. Grabbing the edge of a blanket, I cover myself.

"You are weak for denying the truth between us. Perhaps I chose wrong," I gripe, searching for my clothes.

His growl abruptly ends, and that unnerves me more than any sound he could ever make.

I tense, but the next moment I'm on my front with my hips in the air, his hand pushing on my back while the other bands under my waist. A shriek escapes me, but no one comes. *Is anyone left in the caves?*

When the silence continues, I know we're alone. Had Zaeyr frightened the guards off?

"You have already made your choice, Aida." His hot breath fans my backside. "You made it for both of us. I will show you how weak you are."

Before I can struggle, his tongue lashes hard between my legs. Stunned, his tongue lashes again—twice more—forcing my legs to spread as it dips and tastes every private place I have, shooting waves of pleasure and embarrassment through me. "That is it, human. Submit. Submit like your body begs you to." His tongue finds my core and shoves into me. His words hit home.

"No!" I shriek, ramming back with all my might. "I am the best huntress of my tribe. You will not see me submit!"

Zaeyr falls back, and I find my bone dagger atop my discarded skirt. Grabbing it, I jump on top of him and, straddling him, press it to his throat. His eyes widen as his hands grip my hips. I press the dagger harder.

"Aida," he rasps.

"If you want to mate a human female, dragon, you will mate her in the way she has been prepared." It's my turn to growl. *Elders be damned.* I have earned the right of this choice. "You will submit to me!" I take his girthy cock with my free hand and squeeze it. Rising, wet and dripping, I poise his wide head at my entrance and settle over it.

Keeping my knife to his throat, I push myself down onto his prick. His hands grip my waist. He doesn't stop me.

Wrenching my eyes shut, I work myself onto him. My core expands to try and accommodate his size. When I finally get his tip into me, tears are trailing down my cheeks. I stop, allowing my body to adjust.

"Keep going, human," he orders with a gravelly voice. "Prove your point, or I will throw you back beneath me."

Heat surges somewhere inside me at his words. "You wouldn't dare," I gasp, nearly dumbfounded by the sensations. *I can do this.* I release the dagger and take his girth with both of my hands and work my body over him.

Hurts. Noises escape. It hurts, but it's perfect. I always knew losing my innocence was going to be hard, but this... *This is hard and delicious.* Zaeyr's hands leave my waist to cup my buttcheeks as I begin moving up and down—a little at a time, slowly moving onto his huge girth—adjusting more with each second.

I'm spread wide, stretched. But then I reach my barrier and pinpricks of pain seize me.

I stop.

Forcing my gaze to his, it's wild and ferocious and dangerously heated. A flash of his dragon form surges to my thoughts. My small human form, taking his lumbering dragon's prick, which—in my vision—is nearly as big as I am.

His hands knead my cheeks, bringing me back. Yet it still feels like I'm taking his dragon's body into me. *Too much, too large...*

"Well?" he taunts. "Do you give up?"

"I'm..." I gasp again, shuddering. "I'm at my breaking point."

Something rough caresses my back, and I see his tail move beside me. My eyes widen for a stunned moment.

"Excuses," he accuses, his nails biting into the flesh of my behind.

Shaking my head, I whimper, "Any more and my innocence will tear."

His eyes narrow. "Tear?"

Searching for relief, I move a little up and down his tip, wincing. "I've never been breached before... I'll tear the first time it happens. I may be a huntress, I may be prepared," my voice is breathy. "But you're—you may be too big. I can't." I hate the failure in my voice.

I'm barely aware of his body stiffening beneath me while blinking back the tears on my lashes.

And then, when I start to rise, he thrusts his hips up into me, forcing me to take all of him—breaking me. I cry out and drive upward—sparks shoot across my vision—but he clamps my hips with his hands and traps me on to him.

Oh, waters! My head fills with curses.

Pain and pleasure flood my body.

"Now you have been penetrated, human, by me. And only me."

11

MATING A HUMAN

STRANGLING TIGHT, gloriously hot and deep, I force myself inside my human disregarding her misgivings.

"You will take me now. You will take me until you are seeded," I warn. "The mating heat will not end otherwise, and it will only grow worse."

Aida does not respond.

"The smallest femdragon accepts males twice her size."

She falls against my chest, hands curled into fists, eyes tightly shut. She shakes deliciously. Supple, enchanting. She tries to move off me again and again, but I keep her mounted, knowing it will case. *I will work her until she eases,* I snarl inwardly.

She rubs her slick brow upon my chest. Sitting up, I wrap one of my arms around her and seek her softness, the scent of her flowery sweat.

"It hurts," she whimpers.

"Shhh. Take it, take me."

I slowly start caressing her flesh, massaging and petting every place I can reach without shifting her. Soothing her. My instincts win over my need to punish her.

Before long, the tension radiating from her eases at my coaxing. *Good, human.*

Relax.

My hand pushes down between us, where her core is spread, filled with my thrumming cock, and my fingers discover a strange nub.

She moans and jerks as I pass over it, so I do it again, my cock liking the movement. *If she is willing to submit...*

I need it. Her submission.

I have lost all, but I can gain this. I want this. For endless years, I have wanted the prize of being chosen by a female, prepared my lonely sapphire caves for a future mate.

Tapping her nub, flicking it, my female's moans grow—soft and sweet to my ears. My balls rise even higher, the pressure in my loins builds with each sound. I need her to move, to slide her tight sheath over my achingly sensitive human shaft, but I will not force it, instead working more moans out of her.

She will do it herself when she is ready.

Her brow rises from my chest, and the touch of her lips press to the scales on my torso, she dabs her tongue out to taste them, and mindless hunger floods me.

"Aida," I rasp, against my better judgment, showing her weakness. I rub her nub faster, harder.

Delighting when she flings back and grabs my thighs. Her gasps are music to my ears. Her long hair falls back and tickles my legs.

I like hair, her silky hair, I realize. *I like this human softness...*

Her core clenches. A little seed shoots into her. "See, human," I groan. "You accept me. Now prove your skills." Her nails dig into my legs at my goading.

She lifts herself off me, slowly at first, tensely, then lowers. She does this again several more times, each rise and fall making my teeth grit for control—her tightness a punishment and a pleasure at the same time. But as she continues, her heat and pheromones fill the space between us, and she begins moving faster.

With her head still back, her knees rising where she is straddling, my human finally manages to work herself off my shaft's girth. *Good, human.* Guttural noises tear out of me. Aida falls back down on me with a cry. *YES!*

I cannot help the spurts of seed that streak out with each flutter of her sheath.

"Yes," I growl when she moves faster, taking me in like the huntress she is. Hunting pleasure.

My human rider.

Not on my back, but on my shaft. Shifting my tail between us, I flick her sensitive nub with my tip. Animalistic noises sound from my throat. Her head flips forward, her dark eyes meet mine, glisteningly wet and squinting with need.

My hands grip her hips hard, slamming her up and down my length. She screams and I do it again, taking over.

Pumping into her, my gaze leaves her shocked expression to her bouncing breasts. Her tits are tight and peaked now, begging for suckling. *Another difference between our species I like.* Leaning forward, I capture one honey bouncing tit between my lips.

Aida's hands leave my thighs to claw my back.

I graze my teeth over her.

She scratches me. It is not enough.

My thrusting grows faster. I want to break her in two, need to feel her strangle me and pull out my seed. She is no longer able to keep up with my speed and lets me take over.

I get my submission.

Using her soft yet lean little body, jerking, shunting upward while I force her hard down all to my pleasure. Her cries spur me on. Her arousal grows in the air, and I suck it deep within me, feasting on the smell of her and my seed mixed.

Right when I am about to explode, burying my face

between her breasts,, Aida clamps down hard on me, flinging wildly out of my grip.

Stunned, my eyes snap to hers just as they fall back into her head. Her body shoots up straight, her mouth poised in a silent scream, and her deep grows so wet, so tight, uncomfortable pressure—breathtaking pleasure—clenches my shaft.

Her core pumps, pulling the seed out of me forcibly. I explode, roaring in satisfaction.

She falls into my chest, breathing hard, then going silent as wave after wave of my seed jets out. Seed that has burned inside me for countless years, priming for my mate. I shoot up to my feet, still holding my human to me and keeping her on my cock as my hips thrust and the spewing continues. My tail goes straight and stiff.

I feel her belly expand against mine.

Raw power floods me. *My mate.*

Take me, take it all. It is yours.

When the overwhelming pressure begins to fade and my spurts come to a blissful end, I realize there is something wrong.

Aida is limp in my arms. Her legs have fallen, and she is only held onto me by my grip.

"Human?" I grasp her hair and pull her head back. "Aida?" Her eyes are hooded.

No response.

Any satisfaction dies, leaving shock and worry behind.

"Aida?" I say louder, laying her on the ground, pulling myself out from between her legs. The scent of mating builds, ignored.

She does not move. I put my hands to her neck, her chest— there is movement beneath. Calming down, I lay my ear to her and listen for her heartbeat. *Thump, thump; thump, thump.*

It is strong, but that gives me little relief.

I knew humans were weak.

I did not care, forcing her to accept me anyway.

Sensations of something slimy squeeze my chest. Something I have not felt since a young dragonling.

Guilt.

I throw a clean hide over her, gather her into my arms, and rush out of the cave, searching for anyone who may be able to help. I see sunlight at the mouth of the cave and hasten my steps.

And run head-first into another human.

The human falls back. "Oomph." Muttering, the human rebalances.

"You, help me! She is not responding," I order, laying Aida down in the grass outside the cave. Rain falls from the sky but it is nothing like the day before, a wispy shower. Still, I move Aida closer to the rocks and shelter her as best I can. My guilt grows, seeing her limply lying there.

The other human settles next to me with a gasp. "Aida!" Her hands go to Aida's cheeks.

I hiss low in warning, and the human moves them away.

She turns to me. "What happened?"

"I seeded her," I say, keeping my eyes on Aida.

"Seeded her?"

"Mated her, rutted her if you will, filled her with my seed so she may breed my young." I finally lift my eyes to the female next to me. *How does she not understand? Do human males not seed their females?*

I did not ask. Another stab of guilt hits me. *If my seed kills my mate...*

The other human is staring at me, glancing at Aida before looking back at me.

"Can you help her?" I ask.

"She's my sister. Of course I'll try."

12

DELINA AND ZAEYR

Intensity wells within me and I can't stop it. My aching muscles relax, my core tenses, and Zaeyr's cock pounds me like he's pounding my soul. Any pain or discomfort fades to bliss as the burning heat within soothes it away.

Each gush of his seed brings on another wave, and soon the pain of penetration and stretching is a distant memory.

It's too much to bear, I try to tell him this, but he doesn't hear me, pounding away. Lifting me, holding me against his chest, thrusting in and out, in and out.

Water sluices over my skin, followed by cloth. I moan but can't seem to rise. Settling to the comforting touch of cool water, knowing I might be stunned, I let myself be tended to.

I feel the shift of movement and soon the scent of herbs, wood, and the ocean hits me, and I know I'm no longer in the caves.

Does mating stun? I wonder. I've never heard of such a thing.

It hurts, yes. It's overwhelming. But never once did any of the elder Sand's Hunters women mentioned falling unconscious... *or the amount of male cum...*

Dragon cum. Has to be. It's inside me still, doing strange things to me. Relaxing me in a way I can't resist.

"Well?"

Zaeyr's voice. I try to respond but my lips refuse to move.

"She's fine. Just needs rest. Aida doesn't take care of herself as well as she should."

Delina.

More water is poured onto my skin, and the hands and the cloth that follows are clumsy. It's Delina cleaning me, I note. But then a strand of my hair is pulled behind my ear. The warmth that ignites from it is caused by Zaeyr. I know it.

"How much longer?" he asks.

"I don't know."

"Guess!"

"Let her sleep through the night," Delina answers hurriedly. I don't want to sleep. I want to be awake. I've been asleep long enough... I should be helping my tribe. I want more time with Zaeyr. I can't remember a day in my life when I did nothing but lie in the hides. "When she wakes, make sure she rests. She'll need food too. I can stay and watch over her."

I hear a grumble and nothing else. I'd grumble too if I could. Silence descends between them and I hear the crackle of a fire.

Falling back asleep, I wake up sometime later to Delina's voice. Swimming through the haziness of my mind, I discover she's asking Zaeyr questions.

"...you were a dragon yesterday. I've never seen a dragon or heard of them either until lately. Were you frightening?"

"Mmmm."

"I'm sure you were... Your horns and tail are beautiful. I always envied the merfolk for their tails."

It feels wrong listening in—or trying to at least—without them knowing, but my curiosity is piqued. I don't like my sister speaking to Zaeyr like this, not when it should be me or when

—I'm assuming—they're alone. Trying to rise again, I find there's enough strength to shift my arm a little, but it's not enough to rouse.

"Thank you," Zaeyr mumbles. "What is this used for?"

Delina chuckles softly. "That's a headdress. It's an adornment—" Delina moves "—a female wears during the mating celebration. I wore this not long ago. Here, let me show you." There's a rustling sound. "See? Isn't it beautiful? Those pieces there are the dress and these are the accessories. I could put those on too?"

My heart hammers. What's my sister doing?

"Mating celebration?" Zaeyr asks.

"You don't know anything, do you?" Delina teases.

"Not when it comes to humans," Zaeyr's voice is low and gravelly, almost curious. It floods me with renewed warmth, but also mortification. "Dragons do not celebrate mating," he says. "A femdragon goes into heat, more so during the red comet, and calls out for a male to nest with her. She seeks the best, denies the weakest, and if more than one finds her at the same time, we fight to the death for her attention. It becomes increasingly painful for a male dragon to be in heat from a femdragon's pheromones without seeding. Oftentimes, those that survive a battle for a femdragon will perish without satisfaction. Or, if they are lucky, find a female drake or wyvern of the lesser species to empty their shafts, so they may live."

Oh.

My... that's nothing like humans.

My sister echoes me. "Oh... Males fight over females?"

"Yes."

"That's amazing! I can barely imagine it. To have such a choice..."

"I would not describe it that way. Why do you?"

Delina coughs. "Human males are rare, very rare. The elders between tribes fight for them, and when they come of age, they're given as mates to the most fertile, deserving female of the chosen tribe. We don't have a choice, like your males, I suppose. It's why we celebrate such an event."

My sister's words hurt, bringing back bitter memories of all that happened between us in the past month. How the elders picked her over me when I had been chosen and prepared for the honor and responsibility since childhood.

I don't want Zaeyr to know.

My chest tightens.

But Delina continues, her voice softening. "The elders chose me to be the best mate, the best female. Aida was supposed to be given the honor, but they decided that I'm better able to carry children, perhaps more desirable to a male —the strongest male."

Trying with all my might to rise, blood rushes through me, straining. If not to stop Delina, then to run away. I hear her move closer, approaching where Zaeyr breathes. I would know where he is even if he didn't make a noise. The bond, it's because of the bond.

Even bonded, I don't know if Zaeyr would not take another —perhaps more—if offered. *Would he?*

"Backwards," Zaeyr spits. "Elders should not choose who mates. How can they know what others want?"

"It's not about what others want, dragon, but about ensuring our survival," my sister whispers. "Your survival too. Look at me."

A grunt. "Why?"

There's a rustle of cloth.

"What are you doing, human?"

I want to cry.

"Unlike Aida, who passes out, I know how to mate. I see your cock—it's hard, it can't feel good like that, but I can help. Let me give you relief, and I'll show you what Sand's Hunters chosen female can do. The strongest male should be with *me*. And you are the strongest, are you not?"

"Is this what you human females do? Battle for the best male instead? Even when your opponent is down?" he snarls. "Do you dare to presume that an alpha dragon does not make his own choices?"

My hands finally move. I clench my fingers to my palms, finding the movement difficult but manageable. My eyes snap open and I scan Delina's hut, finding her bare-chested and wearing the mating headdress. She's sitting right before Zaeyr by the fire.

"You understand it, don't you?" Delina hums, reaching up to rub her breasts. "This makes sense."

I look away when Delina reaches for Zaeyr. I wish I was still sleeping. I don't want to see this. Pain constricts my chest.

If Zaeyr allows my sister to have her way, I won't recover. I won't. Not this time.

And what makes it worse, I know, is that I'll still want him afterward, against my better judgment, always remembering that moment on the beach. Even now, the sensation of my innocence broken is there between my legs—the stretching, the needy ache building untoward. His smell fills my nostrils with every breath, making everything worse.

My head falls to the side, pulling my arms instinctively into me when noises I don't want to hear reach my ears. I realize I'm moving. The feeling of betrayal is helping me rise.

"Zaeyr, please," Delina whines as I sit up straight.

Jumping to my feet, I pivot to them.

Delina is sprawled on the ground, legs open and on her back, dark eyes wide, and Zaeyr... He's baring his teeth, his arm on her shoulder over her, eyes wild. They turn to me at once.

My cheeks redden at the sight. My chest is going to explode from indignation.

"Aida," Zaeyr says, dropping his hand from my sister's

shoulder, rising to his full intimidating height. His horns scrap the ceiling, his tail twisting behind him and the sapphire scales on his body twinkling. The sight of him twists my gut.

Knowing that Delina is scrambling up, holding her shirt to her chest, twists me further.

How dare they?

And, though paralyzed, I was right here beside them.

"Don't!" I snap. "You've made your choice. Don't let me stop you now."

The next instant, I'm out the door and running away, my heart unraveling.

13

RED COMET RAYS

I RUN through the village and to my hut, where I hurry to gather my things. I had already been packing for my now-absurd search for a dragon and still have enough to get me safely to Shell Rock, Issa's tribe down the coast.

She offered for me to stay there the day she delivered Leith to us, and I didn't take her up on it. *Idiot.* I wanted to, but finding a dragon—that horrible hope—had been on my mind. Now, I wish I had left with her days ago.

I wish it more than anything.

Pain lances my chest, a cold sting in my veins. *I should've gone with her when I had the chance.* Keeping my tears at bay— *Zaeyr and Delina don't deserve them*—I make for the door and through the thick jungle trees.

Days ago, they were lit up with banana-bee candles for Delina and Leith's mating celebration.

There's branches, broken trees everywhere, some huts are destroyed, the bonfire is in disarray. But my people are all back, cleaning up the mess.

A twinge of guilt stabs at me, asking me to stay, to deal with my hurt like I always do, to put my tribe first, but my body continues to the lift, hands reaching for the lever that rolls it up.

Throwing my satchel on it, jumping before it's even fully to the top, I hear Zaeyr behind me.

"*Aida!*" he roars, seeing me. "Do not go down!" He's a god in fury, like the terrifying dragon he is inside—his long white-blue hair rippling outward—and my hands falter. But the image of him and Delina flashes in my mind and I release the ropes. The last thing I see before the cliff blocks my view is him running toward me. "No!" he yells.

He's still at the top when my feet hit the sand. I tie the rope into a knot so he can't bring it up.

"Aida!" he screams, his dark voice carrying in the ocean breeze. The lift shakes and rattles as I back up and he tries to make it rise. "You will pay for this!"

"Aida, stop!" Delina appears on the cliff next to him.

"To the deep with both of you!" I curse them, picking up my spear and throwing my bag over my shoulder and running down the coast. It's childish, but it gives me satisfaction. Zaeyr's voice carries behind me and I tune it out, knowing that if I don't, I may turn back and allow him to hurt me again.

Rounding the bend—where the cliff walls that keep the jungle separate from the narrowing beach—I run head first into Leith.

He falls backward into the grass, dropping a basket of plants. "Oww!"

"I'm so sorry," I breathe, flustered, helping him to his feet.

He eyes me in the dawning cloudy light. "Aida? You're awake? Delina said you were seriously hurt."

My eyes narrow as I catch my breath. "Why are you out here alone?"

"Delina sent me to get healing supplies to help you," he says, brushing the sand off his legs. "And I'm not alone. Elae and Jye are with me." He points to the water where two mermaids watch us. Bright red and yellow tails rise from the water to wave at me.

"You shouldn't be alone out here, not even with them. What if something came from the jungle? What if a naga was on the hunt?" All thoughts of Zaeyr and Delina fall from my head for a moment as my mother's words about duty return.

"I can take care of myself," he snaps. "I'm sick of everyone babying me. First Issa, now you? I'm not a child!"

Startled, my mouth purses. "That's not—"

"Treat me like a man." He shoves the basket of plants at me. "Here, this is for you. Though I don't think you need it."

"Leith, I'm sorry. The tribe—"

"To waters with the tribes!" he fumes. "I always thought you were better than them, Aida."

"I'm sorry."

He peers at me, and I remember that, just a month ago, Leith and I were going to be mates. The loss I felt when he was taken away... It blooms with the anger coursing through me now, but instead of envy, love settles instead. Familial love, brotherly love. Leith with his boyish features and wavy shoulder-length hair.

The way I feel about Leith is nothing like the way I feel about Zaeyr.

"It's okay," he says, forgiving me. "I should get back to Delina anyhow. She's probably worried about me by now. And you know... you berating me will be nothing in comparison to what I'll hear if anyone else catches me alone." He chuckles, but there's no mirth to it.

My mouth shuts tight. *He doesn't know. Of course he doesn't know. Delina betrayed him like Zaeyr betrayed me.*

Waters, I hate my sister more than ever at that moment. *Leith doesn't deserve this.*

"Aida!" My name bellowed on the wind makes me stiffen.

"What's that?" Leith startles, pivoting to the voice. "The dragon?"

I notice the mermaids both look in the direction my name came from. One of them says, "Dragon?" Their gazes narrow, their tails drop back into the water.

Leith turns to me and gets his answer.

"Is he the one who hurt you?" he asks, voice darkening, pulling a dagger out from a sheath at his hips.

"No, he didn't hurt me," I tell him. "But I've got to go." I hand the basket back. "Thank you for this, but I won't need them." I turn to leave.

Leith grabs my arm. "Aida, what's wrong? Where are you going?"

"What do you mean 'dragon?'" one of the mermaids calls out to us.

"Nothing's wrong. I'm going to Shell Rock for a while." I tug my arm out of his grip. It's much easier than I expect, already used to Zaeyr's strength. *Stop thinking of him!* My pulse races. *Every moment I remain, he gets closer.* I back up, prepare to run anew—

When Leith grabs me by the shoulders and kisses me.

I drop my satchel.

His lips move across mine.

Stunned, again, I do nothing but reel. My body grows cold when his tongue tries to dip between my lips.

This is wrong. So wrong. I push him away.

"I always thought you and I would be mated," he whispers. "I always dreamed it'd be you."

I shake my head.

He continues babbling, but he's drowned out when my name roars through the air, closer now than ever. "*Aida!*" Zaeyr yells. But Leith reaches for me again and I step back. The grey morning clouds overhead break and a streak of dappling sunlight hits us.

"I can protect you from him," Leith tells me, trying to catch me.

The blood-red glow of the comet pierces through the sunlight.

Zaeyr roars, and it sounds like all the thunder in the world booming at once. It shoots straight to my soul. My body floods with heat; my sex gushes. Fear and want rip through me.

I snatch my bag off the ground and turn away.

"Aida!" Both Leith and Zaeyr yell as I flee.

14

THE CHASE

I DON'T KNOW how long I've been running, but I don't stop. I only hope the river is close. When the clouds dissipate, the land turns red and gold. The beach becomes rocks, and I'm forced into the jungle. Energized by adrenaline, I keep going, rushing by lounging crocodiles and through barely-formed spiderwebs.

Every time I consider stopping, I hear feet pounding behind me, the sounds of panting and snarling.

Zaeyr is close. Nerves zinging, I'm the prey.

My heart races, my body strains, and I surge forward, and though part of me wants to be caught by *him*, the hurt inside me prevents me from stopping.

"*Aida!*" he shouts my name again and again like a beast. It doesn't sound human.

Sweat pours down my flesh.

And then the jungle river emerges. The brackish estuary appears. Like a beacon, my pace grows faster, seeing my goal.

If I can just get across it I can lose him. Lose him and think.

Shell Rock is only several hard hours past the river mouth.

As I get closer, so does Zaeyr. Keeping my eyes trained on

the water, I see Elae and Jye waiting in the river ahead. I don't have time to question and throw my spear to the side, diving in, ignoring the bestial growl right behind me; the faint touch of fingers slipping through my hair.

The mermaids grab me and, to my excitement, swim me across the large gape. I'm at the other side within minutes reaching for the shore. But they don't let me go.

"Thank you," I say, trying to pull away. Their hold on me tightens. "What are you doing?"

"We need the dragon," Jye hisses.

"Why?"

"To pay for his crimes."

Crimes?

Hearing a splash behind us, I twist to see Zaeyr closing the distance. *He's fast. So fast in the water.* My mouth falls.

Makes sense. His tail lashes behind him like a propeller.

Elae drops her hold on me and lifts a three-pronged weapon, aiming it in Zaeyr's direction. He stops when he sees it, though his gaze goes straight for me.

His piercingly light eyes are filled with hunger. A haunting, raw, feverish look that pins me to the spot. His usually pale skin is pink with exertion, blue veins pop from his skin, and everything above water is stiff; his horns are straighter than usual.

I sense his savagery as fresh heat jolts between us.

He surges forward despite the weapon, and Elae screams, "Halt dragon! We will give her to you unharmed if you behave!"

"No," I stammer, pulling back. Jye holds me firm.

Zaeyr pauses as the prongs of Elae's triton stab at his chest. My heart stops.

"What do you want, fish?" he snaps. He looks crazy and restless.

If he gets to me, if the mermaids hand me over, I'm doomed.

"You were once the king of the gulf, the Mermaid's Gulf," Elae accuses.

"What of it?"

Elae snarls as if she got her answer. "We have honored you with jewels and gifts for centuries, but you destroyed our home!"

Zaeyr cants his head, his hair falling into his face. It's as if he's just now realizing the mermaids are here at all. I tug again, trying to escape Jye's grip.

"Your home?" he spits. "My home. You were allowed to live in my domain, to be protected by my presence. I have kept the beasts of the open ocean from your waters. It is because of me you prospered with peace. And what did you do to repay me? Jewels and shells to pretty up my caves? When they were already mine to begin with? No, you repay me by trapping me when I roused. To bury me alive!"

Startled, I stop fighting Jye to glance between the mermaids.

"Roused, dragon king? You did not merely rouse—you trembled the seafloor and frightened all that dwelled away! Our homes crashed down around us. So the conchs blared, calling us forth, and we thought the red comet's glow had touched you and sought to stop it, to allow you to slumber," Elae says, pushing the tips of her weapon harder to Zaeyr's chest.

"Stop!" I yell when I see a trickle of blood.

Their eyes snap to mine. Zaeyr takes that moment to swipe Elae's weapon from her hand. He grabs her tail as she flips, darting under the water.

Jye releases me and rushes forward but stops when Zaeyr raises Elae's weapon and points it at her.

I scurry onto the beach.

"You seek vengeance against me now!" Zaeyr screams, curdling my blood, making the mermaids cower. "If you had let me answer the femdragon and not closed off my cave, your precious home and mine would still exist. You brought this upon yourself!"

The mermaids duck their heads.

"Tell your kindred, if they want to live, to leave me be and accept the blame for their actions and yours. You will no longer have a dragon to contend with under your home, and for that, you should be very afraid. I have shown you mercy today. Remember this. I will not show it again." He throws Elae's tail away and she vanishes under the water. Jye follows.

His glowing gaze meets mine and I swallow. He takes a step toward me, and I jolt back. His body is awash in the red comet glow, and it makes him look monstrous, untamed.

It's the first time I've seen him under the comet's light. He's the same but somehow different... frighteningly so. Like the comet's glow has pierced through his flesh and taken over, birthing a creature not of this tropical world.

And the red... The bright, potent red is like hot lava, steamed water, glowing ruby embers between us. A burning sensation surges through me, wrapping around my limbs.

"Do not run from me, Aida," he warns. My spine stiffens. "I will eventually catch you. There is no place on Venys you can go where our bond will not connect us."

"You do not know my tenacity," I whisper. "Or how far I will go to keep my pride."

His brow furrows but he steps closer. Moving back, my hands fist in the sand at my sides.

"Mate—"

"Do not call me that!" I yell, rising to my feet.

The wrinkles of his brow deepen. I don't like the sudden concern on his face. "*You* are my mate," he says.

"In my culture, a mate does not touch another for release! And to do so right next to me? How dare you. How dare you! And with my sister no less."

Concern eases his brow. "Is that why you ran?" his voice lowers.

Opening my hands, I let the sand I collected drop. I want to run; I want him to come after me. I want him to hurt for the hurt I feel.

But most of all I want him to understand. Understand that I am worth everything, that I won't accept betrayal, that if he seeks to punish me in such a way, I will fight him every day for the rest of my life and make my punishment *his*.

"Yes, that's why I ran." I inhale.

"Your sister... she—"

"I don't want to hear it, please." I shake my head. "She's right you know. She is the elder's chosen. Not me. But if you want her, you have to share her, for she's already mated."

The darkness in his eyes returns, and it all but stabs me in the gut.

Taking another step back, I continue, gulping down my pain, "Delina will make you happy."

Unable to wait for an answer, I turn and run, my hurt doubling at mentioning my sister, at giving up so easily. Zaeyr shouts my name but it only gives me the strength to speed up. Ahead the beach turns to rocks. The isles in the water that signal Shell Rock and the lagoon are not much farther away.

It's impossible to get to Shell Rock remaining on the beach —where the rocks became steep and jagged. The only two routes from here are by raft or by a secret path up into the jungle which leads to a hidden ladder down into Shell Rock's lagoon. There will be apes and cats but...

I make for the jungle.

If I can just get there, if I can just get to Issa... she'll know what to do—

Right when I reach the trees, I'm grabbed from behind and thrown to the sand. Zaeyr's saltwater scent floods my nostrils as I gasp from shock.

He presses himself against my back before I can rise. His hands push my hair aside, and his hot mouth covers the back of my neck, opening wide, clamping his teeth on me. Digging my fingers into the sand, a fierce moan escapes my lips. His hips grind hard against my butt.

Arching up, heat ripples through me, pooling between my legs. My body reacts deliciously to his dominance.

It's primal, rabid. Right.

It eclipses all other thoughts. For once, I'm not the strongest, not with Zaeyr. I can believe it's someone else and not me. *Him.*

I can let go.

"Zaeyr," I whimper.

His teeth dig into my nape. He reaches around to cup my brow to keep my face from the sand, pressing on me from both ends.

I stop fighting, giving into his dominion. He gnaws on my nape, unaware that I'm not responding, pinning me with his hips.

His teeth leave my flesh, though his soft lips remain. "No more fight in you, human? Have I won?" he rasps. "I told you I would catch you."

My skin prickles. My mouth clamps shut.

He lifts off me, tosses me onto my back. His tail wraps around my right leg. "Where is my huntress?" he snaps.

"Gone," I gripe.

He sneers. His horns sparkle in the comet's glow.

"Punish me if you will, take me, but I won't give you the adoration you could so easily get from Delina."

"I do not want your sister!"

"Then why were you atop her?" I shout. "Why was she half-naked?"

Several birds squawk and fly into the sky.

"She undressed. I only touched her when she reached for

me and put her wretched hands on me. I was shoving her away."

I want to believe him, I really do.

"Do you think I would so easily leave my mate after our first rutting, when she is seeded and in distress? That I'd leave my mate for another? Dragons do not deny their chosen. It is sacred! I have won you, mounted you, taken away your human innocence, and you think that would mean nothing to me?" He grasps my hair and forces me to look at him when I try to turn away. "You could be carrying my child right now, Aida!" he bellows. "I will not have another, ever, not now that our souls are interwoven."

His eyes brighten, and mine begin to water staring at them. "And if we weren't interwoven?" I whisper.

"I had the choice to deny you. I did not. I could leave, still leave, allow fate to take its course on our lives, but I will not. I could find relief, eventually, from this mating heat," he pants. "But I chose to stay, to deny your ridiculous human ways, and give my seed to you."

"The beach," I gulp. "I wanted to touch you, needed to touch you."

Zaeyr twists his head to the side, staring down at me. Even now, I see his control splitting, the strain of his muscles, his cock near-breaking through the loincloth wrapped around his waist. His words fill me with hope. *I won't deny him.*

But the beach... Did he feel what I did?

"I wanted you to touch me, human," he says.

I inhale sharply.

"I had never seen so much courage. You with your weak spear, standing up to me—an alpha dragon—when I could destroy you so easily. Could destroy this whole coast with nothing but a whim."

Reaching up, I cup his head and lick my lips. He's everything I ever wanted and more.

He's given me a gift I didn't know I wanted—or needed.

My heart constricts. It squeezes in a way that sends more than warmth rushing through me. More emotion than I've let myself feel since before I can remember. I blink back tears.

I wasn't going to cry for him. I don't know now. It's suddenly hard to breathe.

"Do you understand, Aida?" he asks before letting me pull his lips toward mine.

"Yes," I choke. "Kiss me, Zaeyr, before you make me mad again!" I beg, pressing my lips to his.

15

SUBMISSION

AIDA RUBS her lips on mine, taking the last of my control away. I set her back down on the sand and slam my body over hers as she gives me her softness, her submission.

My draconid instincts shout in triumph. But then her tongue dabs out and forces its way into my mouth. Following her strangely enticing human ways, I push my own against hers. Her mewls fill my mouth, and I feast on them, liking this kissing a little too much.

Now that I know why she ran, my frenzy easies, my worries for her safety coming to an end now that she is under me.

Touching Delina? The thought makes me recoil. Aida's sister was not the one who stood up to me on the beach, nor cared for me through the night, nor pulled me to safety during the storm.

Even so, if Aida did not exist, I still would not take Delina to mount. *She smelled of another.* And her childish human wiles— so easy to see through—were deeply unpleasant.

Aida moans. Her lips caressing mine, obliterates all other thoughts.

My painfully tight shaft, bulges with seed, some of it leaking from my cock's tip. I cannot hold it in any longer.

Thoughts of getting it inside her and penetrating her deep, tight sheath consume me.

But as my tongue plunders her sweet mouth, I taste something unusual, something not of her upon her lips. Another? I do not know.

Savagery pummels me. Growling into her, I replace the taste with my own, gnawing, biting, nibbling, licking, until it is obliterated and gone. *No taste but hers will I hunger for! No taste but my own should ever reach her lips.*

When the wrong taste is gone, rising over her, I lift and carry her to the crystalline ocean.

She whines and rubs herself against me. When we are in the turquoise waters that are like a home to me, I dip her body in and soak her with my old territory, knowing she will rule beside me, despite my new form.

"Zaeyr?" she gasps my name, drenched, her eyes searching me curiously. Trickles of water sluice down her curves. My mouth begs me to follow them with my tongue.

"Mine," I rasp. It is all I can say.

Spinning her around, I rip her skirts up and expose her pink human sex. *Like a flower,* I note, dipping my fingers into her. *Like a delicate flower made for one thing only.*

My stem. My thick stem to stab it, ruin it, control it.

Take care of it—for all the years to come.

She shrieks my name when I find her nub and pinch it between my fingers. Essense pools from her deep, where another one of my fingers explores and stretches her. Her arousal hits my nostrils like lightning. My gaze zeroes in.

Her tiny sheath flutters tight around my finger. I like seeing it deep inside her. I like the noises she makes when I play and pump it, touching her everywhere inside.

Grabbing her wet hair, I jerk her head to the side, all the while stroking her still. "Ready?" I rasp.

If she says no, I do not know what I will do. I am pent up.

The comet's aura quickens and sizzles my blood. It takes an immense effort to maintain my control when all I want to do is lose myself in rutting her.

I am afraid I will take her even if she says no.

She nods, swallows. My gaze follows her throat.

Unable to wait any longer, I push her forward onto her hands and knees in the shallow water, lining my prick where my fingers play. Pulling them out, angling my hips, I ram hard into her.

I roar to the sky as she takes all of me, my knot to my base. My ears fill with her screams. She quivers and shakes as I grasp her waist, pulling out to slam back in.

There is no fight this time from my female. She loosens, letting me pummel her, take what I need, and use her. And I *use* her, brutally, unable to hold back. The only thought I had during our chase was throwing her to the ground and exacting my revenge.

I am the one punished. Not her.

Taking Aida is a sublime punishment, but my right all the same. Her body moves with mine, she holds herself up, bowing back when I pull her, falling forward when I thrust home. Each push heats my insides, *she* grips my prick. The sensation of my seed wanting to burst from me builds.

Bowing over her, shielding her, trapping her to me, I wrap my tail around her front and bind her to my body. Her moans are all I hear. My testicles rise.

Clamping my teeth on her shoulder, my back bows. I erupt. *YES!*

She screams out, falls, but I catch her to me, pumping her with frenzy, forcing her to take the lava of my loins. "Take it, human!" My voice is deep, grave. Urgent. "Take it," I order, pumping more and more of myself into her.

I need to get all of me into her!

A forever later—I am spent. My urgency unstoppable.

Aida is weak in my hold, no longer stiff from the work of my mounting, but soft and full of ease. With the water drifting around our limbs, I rise with her in my arms, and carry her back to the shore, to a grassy stretch before the jungle. I stay planted deep in her little flower the whole way.

Easing us to the ground with soft thrusts, obsession fills me. *She is mine. She will take it.*

I would use her through the coming evening and night if I knew her body could take it.

Lifting my head, I scan our surroundings, listening, shallowly rutting her all the while.

When I am sure there are no predators nearby, I do just that, rut her some more—until she stiffens again, moans in the grass, and her sheath clamps. With little seed left to give, I enjoy the possessive human sensation of her keeping me in place, milking me. And when her body softens again, I finally pull out, rolling her over with my tail.

Her glistening dark eyes meet mine. Sweat slickens her brow. Leaning over her, I lick it off.

"You did not pass out," I say, tasting female spice on my tongue.

She laughs softly. "I did. For a few minutes, I believe I did. I don't remember leaving the ocean."

Petting her, I squeeze one of her plump breasts—which is still covered. Pulling down her chest coverings, I span my fingers over the orb. Her skin is many shades darker than mine. Though I am quite pale in comparison to her people, I realize that humans come in many colors and hues like dragons. "You are fine now. I will make sure of it," I tell her, rubbing her tit with my thumb.

For some strange reason, I suddenly want to rub my shaft over them.

She spreads her legs slightly, dips her hand between us and her thighs, and catches some of my seed over her fingers. She lifts it to her eyes. "This," she sighs, "does strange things to me."

We are both feeling strange.

She is so beautiful in the golden twilight that it hurts. It physically hurts. My chest clenches.

I clear my throat. "I have much to share." I am eager to share.

She pins me with her gaze. Her mouth twitches. "Good."

So unlike a femdragon...

Humans enjoy rutting many times over, I note. My cock tightens. *So do I.*

But she wipes my seed on her belly, closes her legs, and pushes herself against my side, and as she rests her head in the nook between my chest and shoulder, I decide not to mount her again. I clasp her to me.

She is much smaller than me. *I must be careful.*

"I'm glad you came after me," she says after a while.

"I will always come for you," I warn. "Make no mistake about that. I grow cold... and desperate when you are not near me." I peer up at the comet above. "It is not a nice thing to feel."

She nuzzles her cheek on me. "The same happens to me, Zaeyr." She breathes my name, and it is wonderful. "Is it the bond?"

"I do not know. And even so, I do not like you out of my sight."

"...Why?"

"I have never laid eyes on something so beguiling as you." It is the truth. "I have seen much—all the treasures of the ocean and more, all the creatures that roam the shores and waters—and none have broken my thoughts like you have, none have upended the wants I always wanted."

In the distance, the sun begins to set. The music of the jungle changes, grows ever more quiet. Pulling Aida closer to me, she nuzzles me some more.

"I thought you were beautiful too," she says.

"Thank you," I preen. "Sleep now, little human. Tomorrow we head back to your tribe, where it is safe. Until then, you are protected with me."

She hums, and shortly after, she settles.

I watch the stars flicker against the darkening sky, finding that for the very first time, I'm soothed and complete. And when the moon reaches its zenith above, I close one eye and rest.

Knowing I have finally caught myself a mate. The best of them all.

16

THE JOURNEY HOME

CRUNCH.

Waking the next morning, I find a pile of fruit beside me and Zaeyr staring at me from a short distance away, awash in the red light of the comet. His face is a mask of hunger, nearly inhuman.

The sharp lines of his jaw glint with sapphire. His thick brows arch. My eyes dip, finding his tail wrapped around his prick, pumping swiftly.

I shiver, remembering our mating. *Seeding,* I correct.

He takes a bite of his own fruit, and I realize that's the sound I hear. Behind him is the ocean, calm and beautiful.

Pulling my gaze away, sitting up—watching him watch me —I adjust my chest coverings and begin to feast on the meal he brought. I'm tickled he sought to provide for me, and as I go through several fruits, I'm happy he did so.

"Thank you," I say when I finish, wiping my mouth with the back of my hand.

The glow in his eyes darkens. He crawls to me, pushes me down, tugs my skirt up, and forces my legs apart. He presses his thick girth to my opening and rams in.

I'm already ready for him.

Though I still burn from the abrupt stretch.

"Say it again," he orders.

"Thank you!"

He slams home, deep and devastating.

Gasping, spreading my legs, hooking them over his hips. It drives my butt into the ground. Each time the thick middle of his prick slips in and out, I moan.

Grunting, he bows his spine and pulls my chest covering down, taking one tit, then the other in his mouth to suckle. I throw my head back, grabbing his horns, and finding the right leverage *there*—I come.

I cry out, and Zaeyr's rutting grows frenzied.

My core clenches wildy. His grunts turn to ragged bellows —then roars. He roars when his seed bursts and floods me. Clamping hard, I take it all, arching my hips and clinging to him for more.

My dragon gives me everything.

Hard, possessive, savage—everything.

Some time later, his thrusting stops, and I'm back to being an exhausted, weak mess beneath him. Rising, he stares down at me, licking his lips. My belly jumps and I tighten my legs around him. Somehow I'm still wanting more.

"Delicious," he rasps.

He carries me to the ocean until the water is up to our chest. Still planted inside me, he uses one hand to wash the dirt and dried cum on my skin. I touch him everywhere I can in return. There isn't a place he doesn't allow my hands to go.

And when the first gulls squawk above us, he releases me, and we walk back to the shore.

"You want to go back?" I ask, curious. I like this time alone with him. Perhaps a little too much.

"It is your home, is it not? Where your family lives?" He runs his fingers through his hair, pushing it back. The action makes me melt. His gaze trails over my body. "Is it where you are most safe?"

"Yes."

"Then we go back."

Though I will miss this time with him without the others, I nod. Going back is the right thing to do.

My tribe needs me. And with Zaeyr by my side, I have everything I want. Everything they tried to take from me.

I keep reminding myself of this as we make it to the mouth of the jungle river, as I climb onto Zaeyr's back and he swims us across at great speed. As he enters me again on the other side, mounts me against a tree, pulls my hair, and grazes his teeth over my flesh, I remind myself of this.

But I'm nervous. The elders don't like having their power taken away.

Will they accept me as Zaeyr's choice? Will they banish us?

Will they try to convince him there's another who is better?

My thoughts drift to Delina—Leith—a surge of anger slices through me. *Will she leave us alone?*

I don't know if I can forgive my sister for what she tried. I understand she's been raised differently from me, but she knows better. *Whether she is the chosen female or otherwise...*

She knows better. I love my sister and am part of the problem with how she's been raised. There was too much focus on me, and I had always suspected that Delina must've been hurt, overshadowed by the attention on me. Now that I've been in her sandals for a time, I can understand her more.

But even so, Delina's always been spoiled. Chastised when she misbehaved, but never facing consequences. If my sister didn't want to do something, no one forced her to.

While I had to brave dark dangers alone...

Shoving Delina from my mind, I study Zaeyr's back before me. It's toned and strong, like the rest of him. *Whatever happens,*

I know he won't leave me. Whatever my tribe and the elders decide, we'll be together.

I'm not alone anymore.

I reach out and take his hand, clasping it tight. He stiffens, glances at my hand, then clasps mine back. His hand swallows mine.

I'm used to being one of the tallest females in the tribe, one of the strongest... *His hand swallows mine.*

Walking next to Zaeyr like this, I find I have to look up to see his face, straining my neck to take in his striking horns. Even when we mate, my feet don't touch when my legs are curled around him. It's a little unsettling that I can take his cock when I probably shouldn't be able to. I eye the hard appendage coyly. Though Zaeyr's put a loincloth back on, his cock is visible.

I purse my lips. *To the deepest waters with you, Delina. He's made for me, not you.*

Lost in my thoughts, time passes quickly. We avoid the few crocodiles we encounter, Zaeyr points out the large fin of a giant mako shark sometime later, and by the time the sun is far past its zenith, the howls of swing monkeys return to our ears.

There hasn't been a dragon's roar or mating call in days. Despite the comet's red hue, everything is returning to normal. Growing antsy, I'm relieved to see Sand's Hunters cliffs in the distance, though my stomach drops too. Now that the animals are returning, so will the deadlier predators. *They'll be hungry.*

Facing Delina and the tribe is safer than facing a hungry jungle cat or prowling naga seeking a nest to lay their eggs.

My fingers twitch, wishing for a spear or dagger, instead feeling Zaeyr's hand.

"Do not be afraid, Aida," he says as if he knows my thoughts.

I groan. "I'm not afraid. I'm tired."

"Have I worn you out so?" he purrs. *A dragon purr?* The sound goes straight to my heart.

I shake my head. "It will take a lot more to wear me out."

"Good—"

"But I am still tired."

He stops and turns to me. "Why?"

I kick at the sand. The scouts of my tribe will be able to see us on the beach. There's no turning back now. I consider it anyway—for a second.

Already, the lift lowers in the distance.

"I don't want this to end," I finally say, pointing between us. "I... like us being this way." Selfish, I am so selfish. "Not having to worry about anyone else, just us. Just you and me. I can't remember a time where I have not worried—greatly—for my tribe." I glance at the rocks, the coming tribemates with torches. "I still worry," I whisper. "But it's been different lately. It's been easier."

Finding the words to convey why I'm hesitant is difficult. *Who am I joking?* Relaying my feelings at all is a tremendous effort. I'm not used to having someone ask after them.

Zaeyr moves to stand in front of me, blocking my view of Sand's Hunters and grasps my chin with his fingers.

"You are a great huntress?"

"Yes..."

"You were once the chosen female of your elders?"

Where is he going with this? I nod.

"You stood up to an alpha dragon when no one else dared?"

Tears threaten to fall. "I wanted you," I tell him honestly.

The side of his mouth twitches. "Is that all, little Aida?"

Ugh. "No. I wanted to make sure my people made it to the caves alive."

He leans forward and rests his brow upon mine, moving his hand from my chin to cup my nape. Shivering, I give in.

"There is nothing for you to worry about," he says softly. "Nothing at all."

"Halt! Aida and dragon, the elders demand to see you! Do not fight us. Lay down any weapons you hold."

I wince—the tribe comes to collect us. Our time together ends.

"What if my family doesn't accept us?" I ask, hurriedly.

"Then we will run away together." Zaeyr doesn't let go of me. Instead, his lips brush my ear. "You have already proven yourself tenfold. If they do not see that, they do not deserve you." He lifts away and turns from me. It's all I can do not to whimper from the loss.

The scouts on the beach move closer, eyeing us with suspicion.

"We will come willingly," he tells them. "We carry no weapons."

A tear slides down my cheek, and I swipe it away at once. My strength returns. Moving to stand beside my dragon, I stare down my female tribemates before us.

17

ACCUSATIONS

WALKING through the village at twilight, no one comes near us, and those who escort keep their spears trained on Zaeyr. Whispers abound, but none that I can make out.

It's not the reception I expect. I expected a fight with Delina, my mother, perhaps the elders. But this? It's so much worse. I tighten my hold on Zaeyr's hand, glimpsing his face.

Unlike me, he doesn't look the least bit worried.

When we reach the elders' hut, I release his hand and enter first, he follows immediately after.

Father, Stagie, Nata, and Drea are sitting around a low table, talking. Mother is there as well—and Leith. Between them is a weeping Delina. Her eyes lift to mine and she cries louder, burrowing in our mother's outstretched arms.

Leith shoots Zaeyr a look of murder. "What is he doing here?" He stands, points, demands.

"Sit, Leith! It is not you who decides who is allowed entry when the elders convene," Tabach snaps. He turns to me and Zaeyr. "Aida—daughter—and Zaeyr, yes? Please sit and join us."

Leith growls but lowers back to Delina's side.

Zaeyr and I join them at the table. Those on either side slide away, rearranging so no one sits directly next to us.

"He attacked me," Delina cries out. "He tore off my coverings and pushed me to the ground! I was so scared."

I gape, staring at my sister.

Finally, I realize what is happening.

"*Liar!*" I hiss. Betrayed again, by my own family this time.

"Enough," Tabach bellows. Delina sniffles, turning now to Leith. I glare daggers.

A terrible, foreboding noise emanates from beside me. We all look at Zaeyr as he rises back to his feet, muscles strained, eyes blazing. He's focused on Leith, and only Leith. "You," he rasps.

Leith cowers but stands, face going hard. "Do you want to fight, inhuman beast?"

Father tries to settle us again, but his words go ignored.

I've never seen Zaeyr look more savage and predatory. It's not how he looks at me in heat or when he rams himself between my legs—no, he reels with fury. Only fury. Grabbing his wrist, tendrils pulsate beneath my fingers. His fury enters me.

"Zaeyr, don't," I beg, confused. He hates Leith with such passion.

"You, male, I know your smell! It was on Aida!" he roars.

The next instant, he's across the table on top of Leith, pinning him to the floor. He's twice the size of boyish Leith, twice the size of me! *He could break him in two.*

Screams ring out, the elders jerk back, and guards surge into the hut to press their spear tips to Zaeyr's back. His tail swipes them away.

The kiss, I realize. *He knows of Leith's kiss.* My stomach pits.

"See! This is what he is," Delina shrieks. "A beast!"

"Let go of Leith!" one of the scouts shouts.

"No!" I scream, jumping up and throwing myself between

him and the scouts, flinging out my arms. They scowl at me.

Unhindered by the chaos, Zaeyr growls. "I tasted you on Aida's lips. Why?" A hush falls over the group. Everyone is poised to make another move but afraid to follow through. Zaeyr's deep voice commands that much intimidation. "Why!?"

Smoke plumes the air.

Rasping sounds come from Leith's throat.

"Do something!" Delina wails. "He's killing him!"

"Don't you dare," I warn the scouts nervously shuffling. Turning to Zaeyr, I place my hand on his shoulder. "He kissed me. That's all. Let him go," I plead.

Zaeyr sneers. "Death!" Leith begins choking.

Delina's crying turns to sobs.

I drop to my knees and grab Zaeyr's hands on Leith's throat. "Please," I beg. "This isn't how humans react," I tell him, trying to keep the desperation from my voice. "If you kill him, you and I are done. We are done." I pull at his hands. "I should've told you. It happened when I ran. But I forgot to tell you. I'm sorry." I see Leith's eyes begin to water. "He's a good male, a kind male. A close friend. Do not do this."

Zaeyr's hands stiffen, and more smoke pools from his mouth and nostrils, but my words make it through to him. Leith's coughing returns as Zaeyr's grip eases. Slowly, he rises and I rise with him.

Delina falls to Leith's side, crying over him.

Curling into Zaeyr's side, he wraps an arm around me, and it's all I can do to not cry as well.

"This way," one of the scouts says to us, and they shuffle us toward a corner. In my periphery, I see the elders relax where they stand by the wall opposite us. His tail comes up to curl around my leg.

"I'm sorry," I tell him quietly. "It happened so fast. I didn't think much of it after you began pursuing me. It meant nothing, nothing."

His fingers slide into my tousled hair. "I will not kill him... as long as it is nothing."

"Kill him!" Delina snaps, sniffling. "You're the one who should die."

I snarl at her. It's been years since our last squabble, and I've grown so much stronger.

"Stop!" Father yells. Delina clamps her mouth shut. Zaeyr holds me back from attacking her. "We are not acting civilized." He slides back into his spot at the table, palming his face. "Delina, take Leith away and make sure he gets what he needs for his throat."

"But—"

"Go!"

I watch as she helps Leith to his feet and they quickly leave the room. The tension recedes once they're gone. Taking my first full breath since entering, I pull back from Zaeyr, just enough to glimpse his face.

He stares at the door with barely contained murder in his eyes. Swallowing, reaching up, I cup his cheeks and pull his face down to mine, telling him all the things I need to say in my eyes.

When he finally looks at me, he softens, but his words are laced with warning. "You are never to be alone with him again. If he attempts to touch you, he will die. I may not be a dragon anymore, but once we have nested with a female, we are not bothered. Once the seeding has been accomplished, we are left alone. Honor," he hisses. "Honor is lacking in this room."

Before he lifts his eyes to the elders, I lean up and kiss him. Zaeyr melts in my hold as he groans and kisses me back—as if everything that had just happened were a bad dream. Soft and desperate and possessive, the kiss is more than just our lips wetting and rubbing against each other. We speak with our motions and so much is said with such a simple action.

Love. My heart expands. I convey it as I did with my eyes, needing him to understand, needing it in return just as much.

Does a dragon love? Does he even know what it is?

Silly questions. I know the answer; I sense his affection and admiration. The warmth of our bond pulsates, grows. My knees weaken. He tangles his hands into my hair and grasps my head. I need our connection as much as he does.

This time together and these moments.

Father coughs and Mother sighs. We finally separate.

Turning, I find them staring at us. Mortification hits and I blush, wiping my lips. But I'm not sorry.

I've never given myself away to affection easily, and here I am... *Hard Aida falling.* Pulling away from Zaeyr's grasp, I move to the table and sit awkwardly. He joins me at my side completely nonplussed and I kind of hate him for it—jealous of his coolness.

Silence falls as everyone resettles at the table. The two scouts with their spears move to stand stiffly by the door. My heart thunders in my ears.

But my spine straightens, and I level my gaze at those sitting across from me.

Mother eyes Zaeyr questionably.

"You summoned us," I snap when no one speaks.

Nata frowns. She looks at Zaeyr. "Can you assure us that you will not attack anyone else in this room?"

"Unless you try to harm Aida or take her away from me, I will not hurt you," he mutters.

Mother coughs. Nata licks her lips.

Father's brow furrows. He looks directly at me. "Aida, are you safe?" he asks.

"Yes. Yes, I'm safe."

He turns back to Zaeyr. "Then we will not take her away from you at this time."

18

MINE

"Delina has accused Zaeyr of assault." The male elder says this, and I scoff. He is Aida's father, I know. I can smell the similarities between them.

Tabach is his name, I remind myself.

He studies me. "Do you deny this accusation... *dragon*?"

Aida mumbles angrily beside me.

Taking her hand, I stop her from coming to my defense. "I deny it."

"Can you prove you did not do this?"

"She's lying, Father," Aida snaps anyway.

My human, who does not even take commands from me. If I did not still smell the other male's scent in the air, I would smile. My instincts urge me to chase him down, punish him, but it is Aida and her clansmen who convince me otherwise.

There is also a more pressing need to slam Aida to the floor and mount her in front of everyone, show them who she belongs to, who *I* belong to. My shaft—though ever hard under the comet—grows harder at the thought.

But logic tells me that will not go well. *Not with humans, anyway. Especially not in front of her sire and mother.*

If we were dragons, it would be different...

Young femdragons in heat were given to the strongest male dragon by her sire and mother to seed, to learn the proper course of mating. *I am that strong male here—the strongest perhaps in all the wilds.*

"Can you prove you did not do this?" Tabach asks, breaking my thoughts.

"Prove?" I ask, snorting out a wisp of smoke. "Can you not smell her? If I had assaulted her, my scent would be all over her."

Aida tenses beside me, and like a wave, I sense her unease at my words. "I was there," she says. "Though I could not see, I could hear. Delina said since she was the elder's chosen female, she should be with the mightiest male."

Tabach sighs.

"Your sister would not do such a thing," Aida's mother—Shyn is her name—says. "Delina has Leith, and by being chosen, she was chosen to be with him and no one else."

"You don't know your youngest daughter well enough," Aida mutters.

Shyn scowls. "Delina may be spoiled, but she isn't stupid."

"She also has not been raised for the duty she's been handed! She doesn't fully understand the importance. When we were growing up, you and the tribe gave all your attention to me, letting Delina get away with whatever she wanted. Now she's making bad choices because she doesn't fear there will be repercussions."

"You said so yourself, daughter—you didn't see what happened! How can you go against Delina so? When you should have been there to protect her?"

Aida's jaw ticks. "Because I was recovering from mating with Zaeyr," she gripes. I watch Shyn's face void itself of color. "I rose within minutes of the interaction. Zaeyr had his hand on Delina's shoulder. And though I didn't know what occurred, he told me he was pushing her away for being touched unwantedly. Considering the things she said, if anyone assaulted another, it was Delina who assaulted him!"

The females glower at each other.

But before they can continue, Tabach interjects. "Did she touch you first, Zaeyr?"

"Yes."

"What happened after?"

"Aida ran, and I chased after her."

Tabach nods. "And you have brought her back to us. Thank you."

"Only for her safety—assuming this place is safe for us. She is mine. We need a place to nest."

"She's yours?" Aida's mother asks.

"Nesting? What is nesting?" Nata adds.

"We have not accepted your claim on my daughter!" Tabach stammers.

I growl. "You have no choice in the matter, old one! She is mine regardless—not yours, not anymore." Aida shifts uncomfortably next to me. "If you knew anything about dragons, it is that once we mate, we remain with them until our dragonling is raised, protecting them, caring for them, nesting with *them* only. No female, femdragon or otherwise, could come between that. Even if she seeks the protection of an alpha male too, there are no others. I seeded Aida—chose her to carry my young—Delina wanted that as well. I denied her, pushed her away." My voice darkens. "She is not honorable for coming to me when she reeks of another."

Silence falls again between the humans. I find I do not like this or them, wanting to take Aida away, understanding now why my little human did not want to face her tribe. *They ask inane questions. I have never been accused of such a thing in my life.*

If I assaulted a femdragon, she would kill me. If not her, others.

"And nesting?" Nata asks again.

"A place to stay during gestation," I snap.

Aida buries her face into her hands.

Shyn gasps. "She is pregnant? How can you know such a thing? It's only been days!"

"If she is not yet pregnant, she will be within days," I warn. "That is how I know."

Some of the elders gaze at me in disbelief, some shake their heads.

"Aida... you are... you know what this means?" Shyn turns to her daughter, saying her name softly. Her face falls. "What are we going to do about your sister? Leith?"

"I don't know," Aida says, raising her face.

"Are you—are you happy?"

Aida smiles at her mother. "Yes."

Tabach, still stammering, flares his nostrils. "We still have not accepted your union."

I snarl. "Do you not listen, human?"

"Father!" Aida snaps. "Enough. We will leave if you don't accept us."

My heart warms at her words. She chooses me over her people, just as I choose her, humanity and all. Taking her hand, I stand, helping her rise with me. My human does not need this, these people. "You do not deserve her," I tell them.

If her people worried about their future, they would not let us walk away. I could help them. I could extend my protection to them, for Aida's sake, for our future offspring.

But no one says a word.

"Come," I tell her. It is time for us to go. Any longer and I may go back on my own words and harm the others. Aida nods, and we head to the door. "We will leave."

With silence behind us, we walk out together.

19

THE FINAL NIGHT

"Wait!"

Hearing my mother run up behind us, I turn and she envelopes me in her arms. Tensing, she holds onto me tighter, and I slowly ease in her embrace. Zaeyr never lets go of my hand. "Don't go," she begs. "Your father will come around. He... he—"

Pulling back. "He what?"

Seeing Mother cry makes me want to cry. I hold my tears back. She's a tough woman, one of the toughest. I've watched as over and over she's held Sand's Hunters together through her grit alone. I realize I've already forgiven her... *Was there anything to forgive in the first place?*

My heart sinks.

"He thinks you're too good for another, Aida. That there is no male the world over that deserves you."

I stiffen at her words, at her touch. "Why would he think that?" Father and I barely have a relationship.

"He sees himself in you. He loves you."

My anger returns and I pull out of her embrace. "Tabach only cares about the tribe."

Mother wipes her tears away. "No, Aida. He may be a hard man, but he is not without softness. All he does is for you and his family, so you may have a home—a place to be proud of."

I finally dare to ask the question I had been wondering all month. "Did he... did he choose Delina for Leith?"

Zaeyr growls at the mention of Leith's name.

Mother's eyes drop for an instant. It's all the answer I need.

Father was the one who broke my heart, not the tribe.

I gulp, pain zipping through me. "Why?" I whisper. After everything, after spending my whole life proving myself...

"Last season," she swallows, straightening, "when we traveled to Shell Rock for the oyster harvest. He had Leith—" Zaeyr growls again "—come to him after seeing the young male kissing mermaids. They spoke at great length."

I remember the harvest; it wasn't that long ago. Issa and I had roamed the isles by her home for pearls—*pearls to add to my mating dress. The dress Delina wore instead...*

We only procured a dozen, but it was a great day regardless, having encountered a lusty merman who followed us, bringing us the prettiest shells from beneath the waves. In the end, he'd been driven off by a sea snake. So Issa and I killed it, bringing home its glittering pink and blue skin to make coverings for her.

It was one of those rare days Issa was allowed to be free of her ward, of Leith. I recall because I wanted him to join us...

He had no interest in hunting pearls. Instead, he chose to sit by the lagoon and sharpen his spear.

"They spoke?"

Mother shakes her head. "I don't know what they said, but his opinion of Leith fell that day. The male is young, fairly untried, and Tabach could not see you with him. That does not mean he will be a great male one day, but today, he has much left to learn."

Confused by the omission, it is not a side of Father that I know. But I know Mother, and she doesn't lie.

I exhale, and with my breath, it feels like all my confusion finally goes with it. All that remains is...

Relief. I didn't know how badly I needed that answer.

Zaeyr grunts, pulling me back under his arm. "It does not matter. Leith is nothing to us. Aida is with me now. If he kisses her again—"

I circle my arm around his waist. "I'm with Zaeyr," I declare.

Mother's eyes finally go to him, and all her softness fades. I hold onto Zaeyr harder, uniting our front.

Relief or not, it's not enough. My thoughts are jumbled.

After Delina was chosen over me, I never thought I'd have a partner of my own. Dreams of having young dashed to pieces. But it's not only this... *Zaeyr is a mighty male. Any tribe would fight to have him.*

And here we are, possibly leaving.

He's done nothing to deserve this treatment.

"Delina is my daughter too, dragon. She is Aida's blood sister," she says stiffly. "But I will have you stay if it keeps Aida here where it is safe. This is her home. And you, you are just one male. If she is with child, she needs to be with her people."

I glance around and for the first time, I notice many of my tribe looking upon us from the shadows. Above, the moon rises, and the eerie glow of the comet rubies the land.

I love them. I love this place.

"Your people do not deserve her," he fumes.

"That may be so—"

"Mother," I intervene, unable to go through another fight, not tonight at least. They stop to look at me. "We will go to the caves tonight and tell you our decision on the morrow. It has been a long few days, for all of us."

"Daughter..."

"Tomorrow," I say, my voice lowering.

She slowly nods. "Tomorrow then. Take this." She hands us a bag strapped to her back. Inside, I find food and dried meat. She steps back and gives us room to leave.

I swallow hard, holding the bag to my chest.

Zaeyr practically pulls me to the lift and lowers it down for us. He leads me to the caves. We light a torch and head deep within, procuring hides from one of the stashes and setting up a cozy camp by the water.

When we finally settle, I glance at him. He's staring at me with an unreadable expression.

"I do not like it when you hurt," he says, reaching out and tugging me into his arms.

Lowering my head against his warm chest, I let him hold me.

"What do you want to do, little human?" he asks.

"Nothing, not right now. Nothing but lie with you."

"That," he exclaims, holding me even closer, "I would be happy to oblige."

Tomorrow.

Tomorrow, we will choose to leave or stay.

"Do you forgive me?" I ask. "*Can* you forgive me?"

"There is nothing to forgive."

There is everything to forgive. *I brought him into this mess, into humanity, into our looming extinction, into my family...*

But his hands go to my hair, his fingers caress my scalp, and with nothing but the sound of his heart beneath my ear and the crackle of torchlight, I push all concerns from my mind and fall asleep in my dragon's arms.

20

LOVING A DRAGON

I WAKE to find Zaeyr between my legs, licking my sex. A shocked moan escapes me, and I spread my knees. Long fingers slide up and through my private place, where he explores and plays.

I don't know what time it is, whether it's morning or still night. All I know is his sharp tongue ramming into my deep place and his dark groans. He spans his hands and gropes me everywhere.

"Time to breed," he groans, rearing up like a wild beast over me. I lift my hips as he spreads me out and open. The hard tip of his thick prick nudges my opening. His eyes glow bright upon me, lighting the space with blue.

I'm barely ready, but he thrusts, pinning me to the hard ground with his hips. I scream, stunned by being spread so abruptly.

Gasping, he slams slow and rough, each shunt a beating of my body to his—to the floor. Slower still, I'm fluttering and clenching, pushing him out as much as trying to keep him rooted.

I hook my legs over him, once again finding my feet unable to connect. I strain my neck to look upon his face.

But he's over me, his huge body not even arching so our lips can meet. I kiss his torso and chest to get his taste in my mouth.

Thrusting faster now, he snarls like an animal. *My dragon.* And with a roar blaring out, he shoots his seed.

Heat pools into me—so much heat—and I clamp my sex around him. My thighs grab what they can while I cry out. His seed spreads slick between us as he forces me to take everything. And when I'm about to wilt with exhaustion, he releases me.

"Zaeyr," I moan, curling to my side, the sensation of his cum spreading throughout my body. Like the first time we mated, my body shudders, paralyzing me on contact. But I remain conscious this time.

Relighting the torch, he picks me up and carries me to the cave pool, tugs off my remaining coverings, and slips us into the cold water together.

"You are ovulating, human. Your pheromones have sweetened this night," he groans, moving his hands all over me. "It is maddening, and I am *already* mad."

Ovulating? My heart skips a beat and I find the strength to whisper, "What does that mean for us?" I ask coyly, allowing him to move me, wash me, pet me. I couldn't stop him even if I tried. My body is still weak.

"It means we should stay here until it is over, so I may have you whenever I want. I may not be able to control myself."

Oh.

The answer. The tribe. Father... everything comes back to me like a speartip to the heart, taking away the headiness of the moment.

For a time, there's stillness between us.

He hums low, almost in warning. "Do not think of them."

"I can't help it."

"It is because they are important to you." He sighs.

Swallowing, I close my eyes. "Yes." No matter how hurt or angry I am with Delina. My tribe is and always will be one of the most important things to me in my life. If this journey of surrendering a future with Leith has proven anything to me, it's this.

"We will go to them soon," he grumbles, and I ease up against him.

"Thank you." I mean it. So, so much. "I will make this better," I tell him for his sake because I still feel guilty. "This thing with Father, and Delina, will be nothing soon. I promise."

Zaeyr pulls me from the water, wraps a clean hide around me, and helps me back into my clothes, tying the strings, adjusting the shells and teeth adorned on them. It's such a kind, unexpected move on his part that my throat tightens. All my strength has returned by the time I'm ready. He dresses in his loincloth. Finding a cape in the nearby stashes, I pull it around his shoulders and button it at his torso.

Stepping back, the only word that comes to mind is dashing. *My dragon is handsome.*

Wrenching my hands at my sides so as not to touch him again, I know the time has come for us to leave the cave.

We make our way to the entrance, bringing the torch to light our way, ditching it when the dawn's light brightens the path.

The smell of the ocean fills my nose, the sea breeze whips my heavy hair away from my face. Zaeyr takes my hand and leads me into the light. We stand there for a time as our eyes adjust to the light shining down and the brilliant blue skies above.

"Not even a wisp of cloud," I murmur as it all comes into focus. "It's as if the storm never happened at all."

"It happened," he mutters.

I turn to him. "What do you want to do?"

He knows what my question means, what I'm inferring.

"I want to build a nest with you, human, and cover you in my protection." He glances toward the turquoise water beyond the rocks. His face falls and I frown. "I had a nest built, a sapphire and pearl cave filled with all the jewels of this gulf within, with walls that were high and tunnels that ran deep—all for my future mate. Hundreds of years of my life, I prepared the space, waiting."

My throat strangles further. "Under the mermaid kingdom?"

He nods.

"It sounds beautiful."

He looks at me. "It was. It was all for you."

"Zaeyr..."

"Do not," he hisses. "I have a confession to make myself, Aida. Several, in fact. I know you harrow with guilt because you touched me, but you should not. You may have sought a dragon for a mate, but you did not seek me out specifically, and I gave you no choice. That day on the beach... I was searching for that other dragon that arrived—a rare femdragon in heat—but when I saw you... It was you who stole my mind, my heat. She wanted to destroy you but I would not, could not let her. You were already mine."

Swallowing, I try to turn away, but Zaeyr reaches up and cups my cheek, rubs my lips with his thumb. *Too much. Too much, dragon. Don't make me fall. I don't know how I can possibly feel any more love for you... It's already overwhelming.*

"Your touch..." His voice softens. "I wanted to hate you for everything you stole. My instinct was to punish you, to force you to be mine, to break you—not once thinking of who you were or might be to your tribe. Maybe it was the bond, or maybe not, but I could not hate you, not even from the beginning. And I tried, human, oh, I tried. I realize now those feelings never came because you gave me everything that I ever wanted: someone to spend my life with. Someone to banish away all my years of loneliness."

I press my cheek into his palm and try hard to keep my tears inside.

"I was so lonely," he chuckles, drawing my gaze back to his. "I spent countless years building a nest for what? Hope? I am glad it is gone, human, because it would only be a reminder of the past." He leans down to press his brow to mine and I shutter my eyes. "So when we return to your people, know that I do not care what choice you make, whether it is to stay or for us to leave."

"I love you," I gasp. I can't help it. My chest hurts; his words constrict my soul. I can no longer keep my emotions at bay. Inhaling deeply, the ocean and Zaeyr's scent pulls into me. It's beautiful—it's home.

"Love?"

"Yes," I whisper. "I love you." I don't care if he says it back. It wouldn't change a thing.

"Is that this overwhelming heat in my heart that makes it heavy when I think of you?" he asks.

"Yes..."

"The need to see you all the time or I may perish?"

"Yes."

"I love you too, little human."

My chest explodes and I slam myself into him, curling my arms around his large form. He picks me up and takes my mouth. His primal taste fills me to the brim.

This, I realize, this is what we both have been waiting our whole lives for. No one can take this away. No one can take us away.

21

A FUTURE FULL OF DRAGONS

THE TRIBE'S abuzz by the time we're pulled up the lift. Several rafts are docked on the beach, half unpacked with supplies.

If my heart couldn't thunder anymore with contentment, it still does, knowing those rafts are from Shell Rock.

Issa!

I'm nearly bouncing on my soles by the time the lift tops the rocks. Strangely though, Zaeyr goes rigid beside me, and when I glimpse his face, his cocky smile is gone. He took me again against the rocks outside the cave, quick and loving, whispering the word against my skin like he was branding it to me, unto and into my flesh.

But any happiness is gone.

Then I see Issa. Beautiful, dear Issa, my truest friend and huntress soulmate laughing with Leith by the central bonfire. Her long braided blond hair shining in the sunlight, her gold-kissed skin dressed in nets and white shells.

"Issa!" I yell, catching her attention as I rush forward and envelop her in my arms. She's tense for a moment, and I wonder if I've ever given her a hug in the past. *I'll rectify that.* "I'm so glad you're here," I cry.

"Aida," Issa muses. She eases into my embrace and hugs me back. "I was so worried. Waters, I am relieved to find everyone okay. I could barely sleep with worry."

We grip each other once more tightly before pulling back. I'm taller than her by several inches, but Issa knows how to use her shortness to her advantage, especially when we wrestle. I know to never underestimate her.

"You were worried?" I ask, finally registering her question.

"I saw the alpha dragon..." Issa's blue eyes trail behind me and she stills. Turning, Zaeyr is as tense as ever standing nearby. Leith is several yards away looking on worriedly, having backed up, but as I glance around, I find what Zaeyr is staring at, it's another large male.

A large green male.

My mouth drops.

A large green male with wings on his arms, emerald and jade scales covering portions of his body, and long snake-like black hair. He's looking at Zaeyr the same way my dragon is looking at him: with blatant suspicion.

"Me," Zaeyr says. "She saw me."

I turn back to him. "You?"

"When I emerged from the sea, I sought him." He points to the dangerously ripped green male behind Issa. "And saw her instead."

"Yes," Issa whispers. "You're him, the alpha dragon from the ocean..." She shivers. "The one in the storm."

The other male finally speaks. His voice deep and gravely. "Where is the femdragon?"

We all turn to him at once.

"I pushed her against the cliffs, forced her away. She fled into the clouds. She has not returned since, near mad with unrelieved heat," Zaeyr tells us. "And since she has not come back I can only assume she has taken a lesser beta or omega draconid to nest, or that her heat has passed and she slumbers. I do not sense her."

"Nor do I," the other male grumps.

"And if she comes back?" I ask. I hadn't thought about that happening, not once. My palms slicken.

Zaeyr finally drops his eyes from the other male. "We will send her away or help her find a mate nearby."

"Yes," the green one agrees.

A cough has the four of us turning again. Mother is standing off to the side holding a platter, eyeing all four of us, and it's then I realize the buzzing tribe has stopped to watch our exchange. Half I know from Shell Rock, and they gaze at Zaeyr with wonder, while my tribe watches the other male.

Dragons. Two of them. No one needs to tell me the other is a dragon as well. *So Issa took stock in the rumor I told her.*

Mother comes forward with a platter of baked fish, fruit, and raw oysters. Issa takes it from her, and we settle around on driftwood seats beside the fire. My friend sits with the other dragon male, and his wing flutters out to caress her side.

They are bonded. It's unbelievable. *My dear friend has found a dragon of her own.*

Despite Zaeyr's growl, Leith slowly joins us and lowers between Mother and Issa—the furthest place possible from Zaeyr. While we eat in awkward silence, the tribe returns to their laughter and talk, others come to join our gathering.

They're waiting for my decision. Mother's gaze falls on me again and again.

I don't know how much Issa and her dragon know, but they remain courteous, eating. Zaeyr is tense or terse, or both.

Leith asks how Issa and her dragon met, and they tell us their story.

"I stumbled upon Kaos—" *the other dragon's name is Kaos* "—when he awoke in the Forbidden Jungle," Issa says.

"She touched me," he adds.

Issa chuckles. "Many times, actually."

"We are bonded."

"Oh yes, that," she chuckles louder.

"She is pregnant with our first young."

Shock falls upon the group.

Mother speaks first. "So it's true? This bond, this fertility? You know you are with child?"

Kaos nods. "I sense him."

"Him?" Mother gasps.

Issa wipes her mouth. "Kaos is very sure of his abilities." She shrugs.

"Are you two... happy?" Mother asks.

Tulia, one of Issa's half-sisters, joins us and sits down. "So happy it's sickening. I'm sickened daily by it." Tulia laughs anyway. "But our tribe could not be more joyous. I have not seen our people so hopeful in many years. We were ended, and now... Now we are not."

Leith pipes up for the first time. "Sister, I'm so thrilled for you. I will be an uncle! I look forward to the day."

Issa beams.

Envy strikes me. I clutch Zaeyr's hand and squeeze it. He squeezes mine in response. *Does he sense young too? Will he know when I'm with child?*

Father comes to join us at some point.

Delina never shows.

I watch as my friends and family talk and laugh, ask and answer questions, continuing until the food is all gone and nothing but spirits are left to pass between us. Even Zaeyr lets up after a time, and his watchful stare on Kaos eventually comes to an end. Kaos's glares cease as well.

Whatever it is between them, is gone for now. Knowing all that I know, they were rivals in a way, at some level, but now there's nothing for them to rival about. I hope.

Happiness returns and I realize how much I enjoy this. I've

already made up my mind, but now it's just to tell Mother and the others. Issa and Kaos helped me make up my mind. Seeing them and their tribe so happy... It proves that things can be better—will be better. Change is never easy.

Somehow we've been at this all day. And as the sun begins to lower to dusk and the comet's rays ruddy the land, I clear my throat.

Mother, Father, Leith looks at me. I hold their gazes. "Zaeyr and I have decided to stay. As long as we're together." We won't let them force us apart. They can keep us as is, or not at all.

Finally, some pressure lifts—it vanishes completely when Mother smiles. I can't help but smile back at her. Excitement for the future and everything it will bring with it fills me.

Father raises a cup of spirits, clapping it against Zaeyr's—it's more of a response than I could've asked for—and we all raise ours in celebration.

Then Issa, Tulia, and even Milaye grab hold of me and drag me to my hut.

22

MATING RITUAL

WATCHING my mate get pulled away, I stop myself going after her, calmed by the laughter and the grin on her face.

I have never witnessed such happiness. *Her tribe is not only a place of safety but community too, and love. The love she offers so sweetly to me.*

I am beginning to understand humans. They are not at all the wretches we dragons make them out to be. If they can survive this world, like us, they must be great in their own way. Intelligent, emotional, strong...

As Aida disappears with her tribe's women, my eyes drift back to Kaos.

Even from where I sit, I could sense the young in the belly of Kaos's female—its life. Though now she is with Aida, I no longer feel the child.

To be so near another alpha dragon's young and his mate— for him to be so close to mine—is unheard of. But here we are, humans both, not trying to kill each other. Succeeding.

Kaos notices my gaze and leans back. Stiffening, I watch him rise and move toward me. He keeps his wings retracted. I keep my tail relaxed in response. He sits.

"Good journey, ancient one," he says.

"Good journey," I tell him back. Kaos is an alpha dragon too, but younger than me. He is a dragon born of two other elementals: Earth and Water, and it is his water half that aligns us. Somewhere, far back in our ancestry, we may have shared a relative, but with so many years between then and now, we will never know.

Though, I wonder...

We sit in silence for a time watching the fire. Fire that, at one point, lived in our bellies. It grows as more wood is added, fighting off the coming twilight.

"You did not answer me that day I roared for you," I muse at last.

He shrugs. *Such a human gesture.* "I had no reason to," he answers.

I try shrugging myself. "It is for the best."

"Yes."

"You kept your wings," I say.

Kaos hums. "You kept your tail. I say we are equal."

I find myself chuckling. "Are we though? Really?"

"Perhaps we will find out in the years to come," he muses. "Perhaps we will never know. I do not think our mates will like us battling."

"You may be right."

"I know I am. Aida is your mate's name, is it not?" he asks.

Hearing Kaos say her name makes my heart pound. "Yes."

"Issa has been worrying about her often since the storm. She was afraid you might destroy Sand's Hunters, Aida and Leith with it."

I stiffen, snarl. "Leith."

"You do not like the young male?"

"He kissed Aida."

Kaos growls. *He understands.* Dragons do not share, are deadly possessive and protective of their mates for as long as they have them. And I know, when it comes to human females, we will have them forever.

Growing antsy, my gaze goes to the hut Aida entered. *Where is she?*

Issa is gone too. Kaos must sense my unease. "Do not worry. She will be out soon. They are preparing her."

I glance his way. "What do you mean?"

"Just wait and see. It will not be long now." Before I can inquire further, he rises and returns to his previous seat. My attention returns to the hut. My brow furrows.

An eternity passes before the door opens. Or maybe several lengthy minutes. And it is then I realize that the entirety of Aida's tribe is around me and the bonfire.

The three other females appear first. Milaye I already know, and Tulia I believe to be second. Kaos's mate is third, smiling big. Her bright eyes find Kaos and she goes to him.

I wait for my Aida to emerge.

Preparing her for what?

When she doesn't appear, I rise, planning to seek her. But then a shadow fills the doorway and I see her.

My feet stop mid-stride, stunned.

Aida steps from the threshold and into the evening glow. Awes fills me to see her in such a mesmerizing way.

Enchanted, her dark eyes catch mine, and I am lost. The firelight spark and even a glint of red shine in her gaze, all framed by black chalk that goes from her eyes to her hairline. My mouth waters.

Her long, beautiful hair is pulled away from her face, sharpening her features, hanging down her back in enticing waves. A twilight goddess of golden sands. Or a seductress coming from the deepest fires of the earth.

My eyes slip to her body. Her skin has been donned in glittering shells, gold and twinkling. Adornments go up her arms, her legs, even her fingers and toes have accessories—intent to seduce my gaze everywhere at once.

I wipe my mouth with the back of my hand. I do not even try to hide my shaft, threatening to slip from my loincloth. She is dressed in dark green snakeskin that barely conceals her sweet parts. White pearls are sewn over her breasts and the crux of her sex. Pearls I want to tear off with my teeth. *My water nest was filled with pearls.* Forcing the thought from my mind, I vow to procure new ones.

Aida takes a slow step my way, her teeth bite down on her lip, and I am paralyzed. My nostrils flare. Her pheromones flood into me. I realize everyone else is watching her too.

We should have never left the caves! A rumbling grows in my throat.

My shaft grows painful, and I want to throw her over my shoulder and take her away at this very moment. *Or remain here, in front of all, so they might witness my mastery.* My mind clouds with lust.

I hear laughter. I do not care. Clenching my fists, I straighten, ready for my human to close the distance between us. But when she is only a few yards away, she is interrupted.

"Wait!"

Holding back a scowl, Delina runs up and forces Aida's attention from me. Breathless, the younger sister raises something in her hands.

"I'm sorry," she whispers, offering the object.

Aida glances down at it, back to her sister. Forgiveness softens her striking face. My mate nods and lowers her head. Delina lifts the object and places it on Aida's head.

The headdress, I note, realizing what it is.

Delina positions the piece and ties it into my mate's hair. Their brows touch, and then Aida turns back to me. Delina slinks away.

I do not wait any longer—can not wait without going mad

—and storm across the clearing and take her in my arms, slamming my mouth over hers.

Like shrugging—no, it's better than shrugging—Kissing her is such a human mannerism. One I enjoy immensely. Something I will enjoy every day for the rest of my life. *No one will ever again kiss her but me.* I nip Aida's plump lip, and she pulls back with a gasp.

The tribe breaks out in hollers and laughter, and without caring of whatever human ritual we are in, I pick my mate up, throw her over my shoulder, and steal her away.

My human.

My. Human.

Mine.

EPILOGUE: AIDA'S PARADISE

THREE YEARS later

"Should we go deeper?" I ask, gazing at the shadowy passage leading further into the jungle.

"Yes!" Gullis exclaims with a squeal, waving his little dull spear that Kaos, his father, crafted for him.

"I want to see!" Haime cries with him, holding onto my hair, leaning over my head where she's perched.

My daughter. My beautiful daughter with blue eyes like her father, shadowy skin like mine, and sapphire scales now appearing across her skin. Her sense of adventure keeps me alert—terrifies me hourly. Her little tail swishes against my upper back.

Issa sighs behind me.

For the first time in years, neither she nor I am pregnant.

Thank the waters.

Zaeyr grunts and, with his double-edged spear, breaks the vines in our path.

Kaos strides from behind Issa, our children, and me to join

Zaeyr at the front. Gullis imitates his father and strides next to him, only to fall behind and scurry back up. He takes after the jungle dragon, scales, green skin, and all. All but the wings on his father's arms.

Issa has two sons, and I two daughters. Both of our young babies remain in Shell Rock, Issa and Kaos's home, where they're being taken care of by the villagers. I miss them. I've been away from my baby girl for a day, and I miss her deeply. She may be growing horns, and I'd hate to miss their breaching.

"Mommy," Haime whines as she pulls my hair, and when I glance up, I realize the others are all ahead of us. Hurrying my steps, I catch up, ducking through the broken vines fast enough so Haime can't grab them.

But when we break through the passage, they've already reached the rocks to my left. Kaos yells after Gullis, bringing a smile to my face.

We're close. We must be close.

The canopy soon opens up and bright blue skies fill my view. In the distance, my ears prickle with the sounds of waves crashing against the shore.

"Mommy," Haime says again, "we're falling behind." She squirms, fighting to get down from my shoulders, but I grab her up against my chest and laugh. When she giggles, I stick my tongue out at her.

"We're taking our time, baby."

She doesn't care. Fights me again. But I lift her back onto my shoulders, and she settles when I move into the open light to begin ascending the rocks.

This is our first outing as a family, our first hunt, our first real adventure. And we chose to do this with Issa and Kaos and Gullis because it would be a first for them too. *Our dragons work well together when they have the same goal.*

And of all places, we decided to venture past Shell Rock,

follow the coast north, up the peninsula, to where the Mermaid Coast—the Mermaid Gulf—meets the open ocean.

I've never seen the ocean. The real ocean. The vast blue that goes far beyond Venys, endlessly.

I catch Zaeyr looking down from above, watching our ascent with keen eyes. Standing like a god on his perch. *Never a moment he's not there.* I shoo him away with my hands but he remains.

Peering up at him, half-scowling, I can't believe it's been three years. *Three years.*

The world has changed.

Since then, the red comet vanished, Delina and Leith had a daughter of their own, and the beginning of the next generation of our people has been born. My relationship with my sister was at first strained, but since our pregnancies and our young being playful cousins to each other, the past has become the past. It's reminded us of our childhood, of all we've gone through together.

Delina has grown much, and anger is too hard to maintain. Although Zaeyr still growls at Leith and won't let me near my brother-in-law, we remain friends.

I tickle Haime's feet, and she squeals with laughter, bringing a rare smile to her father's stoic and broody facade.

Since then, the mermaids forsook Sand's Hunters for me mating him, for Sand's Hunters giving Zaeyr a home. But I don't think they went far.

In recent months, the babies have brought the mermaids back to our shores. I've discovered the laughter of babies draws in mermaids. Much more so than singing.

Krakens and other enormous leviathans have also returned to the gulf. *Perhaps the mermaids forgot the protection Zaeyr once gave their underwater lands...*

Now he protects the coast, and the shores are safer than before.

The femdragon never came back.

Issa claims she saw a small dragonling fly through the skies, but I don't know...

Makes me wonder...

Reaching the top, Haime whimpers to be on her father's shoulders. Zaeyr scoops her from me and spins her around.

Stoic and broody. I laugh. He looks that way but he's anything but. I curl my arm around his side and lean my head against him. "You didn't have to wait."

"I wanted to."

I pat one of the three bone daggers hooked at my hip and then the net tied to my waist. "I know these lands and its predators better than you, dragon man," I humph.

"But I have better hearing, smell, and eyesight, human."

I humph again and move away.

But he catches me, pulling me into his chest, wrapping his large arms around my torso—shunting his hips against my back. My core clenches. *He wants me. He always wants me.* Smiling, I wiggle my backside.

Perfectly unaware of our silent communication, Haime's little hands reach around her father's horns to tangle back into my hair. "Where's the ocean?" Completely unaware of her parent's tension. My smile grows. Turning around, I tug on her leg.

"Can't you hear it, little seashell?"

Her ear pricks—literally pricks up. Something else she inherited from her father. "I hear it!"

"It's close," I say. "The louder it gets, the closer we are."

"Aida! Come see!" Issa yells from up ahead.

Please let us be there, I beg. *Please.*

Together, Zaeyr's hand in mine, we make our way to Issa's voice.

The last of the brush clears, the sky spans outward, and

after scrambling over several more ledges of rocks, the ocean comes into view.

Sapphire waters stretch out in all directions before me. Water so dark, so deep, a shiver for its greatness courses down my back.

Zaeyr's home. I squeeze his hand tightly.

"Do you think there are others like us?" Gullis asks softly.

Issa licks her lips and glances my way.

"Yes, sand dollar, far north past Haime's home, there are others like us."

The rumor that started it all.

"I want all the world to be like us."

"Me too!" Haime agrees. Her little tail catches in my hair.

Zaeyr hums. "You will have to find a dragon of your own, little one."

"I will!"

"I'll find one too," Gullis announces.

The four of us adults share a concerned look.

"Not today," Issa says, swallowing.

"Nope, not today. Or tomorrow," I add.

"Or next week," Issa continues.

"Maybe next year," I laugh.

"Ugh."

It's something that's been on my mind too. Are there others like us out there? Dragon and human, bonded? And if there are, how many? Where are they?

Zaeyr tugs me against him as a flock of eagles soar by. I lean into him again. *It doesn't matter.*

We stay up on the ledge until the sun begins to set. We make camp and tell stories. The children play, wrestle, and fight. They eventually fall asleep, Haime's tail curled around Gullis's ankle.

I'll never really know if there are others.

And that's okay.

Venys is a big world, after all.

Zaeyr places his hand on my stomach, pulling my attention back to him. When our eyes meet, his flash, bold, bright, and blue. A dark, hungry look I know so well.

I don't need to search for others, because this is mine, it's everything I want. More than I could have ever hoped for.

My heart swells. I'm ready.

AUTHOR'S NOTE

Thank you for reading *To Mate a Dragon*. If you liked the story or have a comment, please leave a review! And if you haven't already, keep on going with Tiffany Roberts, Poppy Rhys, and Amanda Milo's amazingly sexy dragon books in the *Venys Needs Men* series.

If you love cyborgs, aliens, anti-heroes, and adventure, follow me on Facebook or through my blog online for information on new releases and updates.

Join my newsletter for the same information.
Naomi Lucas

Turn the page for the blurb for To Touch a Dragon, Issa's story.

TO TOUCH A DRAGON

The tribes have wilted. The last of the menfolk have grown old. The human race has been dying since the red comet first soared through the skies above.

As the youngest hunter, and the only one left within child-bearing age, I'm doomed to be the last matriarch of my people. Which would be a great honor, if there were a male to be mine from another tribe. But none have been born, none but my younger brother. It's been my life duty to protect him.

When the time comes to escort my brother to a neighboring tribe, my friend tells me a rumor of a huntress finding a dragon in the northern plains. And when that huntress touched the dragon's hide, the beast transformed into a virile, possessively bonded male.

With a thundering heart and nothing left to lose, I venture into the forbidden jungle to find such a dragon. To touch him, to take his seed, to bear his burden.

But the dragon I find is nothing at all like I imagined...

VENYS NEEDS MEN COLLABORATION

VENYS NEEDS MEN

To Tame a Dragon by Tiffany Roberts
To Seduce a Dragon by Poppy Rhys
To Desire a Dragon by Amanda Milo
To Enchant a Dragon by Amanda Milo
To Touch a Dragon by Naomi Lucas
To Mate a Dragon by Naomi Lucas

ALSO BY NAOMI LUCAS

Stranded in the Stars

Last Call

Collector of Souls

Star Navigator

Cyborg Shifters

Wild Blood

Storm Surge

Shark Bite

Mutt

Ashes and Metal

Chaos Croc

(Book 7 Coming Soon!)

The Bestial Tribe

Minotaur: Blooded

Minotaur: Prayer

Venys Needs Men

To Touch a Dragon

To Mate a Dragon

Valos of Sonhadra

Radiant

Standalones

Six Months with Cerberus

Printed in Great Britain
by Amazon